FLYING WITH THE EAGLES II

To ~~Benedette~~ :

Enjoy!

Mary Trask

FLYING
WITH THE
EAGLES II
LEARNING THE WAY

Mary Trask

XULON PRESS

Xulon Press
2301 Lucien Way #415
Maitland, FL 32751
407.339.4217
www.xulonpress.com

Printed in the United States of America.

ISBN-13: 978-1-54566-369-1

DEDICATION PAGE

This second book in "The Flying with the Eagles" series is dedicated to all those seeking peace and answers in the midst of difficult situations. Let me assure you that there is real peace and perfect answers to whatever you are facing found in the real-life El Emet through the only one who makes a way for us, Chen, the grace-giver. The truth is very present, but it is only discovered when one is willing to completely let go of everything in their lives. Once everything is surrendered and the way, the truth, and the life is invited in, all things change for eternity. A whole new and "uncommon way" will be revealed that will release the real you to enjoy the true life you were designed for.

ACKNOWLEDGEMENTS

I would like to thank my husband, John for the many ways he supported and encouraged me in writing this second book. His excitement and enthusiasm inspired me to keep writing this tale exactly as I saw it before me. I would write and he would read. At the conclusion of each chapter, he would call out, "More, more!" I loved it! At the conclusion of the initial writing process of this book, my dear friend, Dori Olsen would come over and spend hours with me refining my descriptions and sentences so as to appropriately capture this story. Thank you, Dori! I would also like to thank the very gifted illustrator, Sam Wall, (www.samwall.com) who diligently worked with us to capture the right look for this exciting account on the fictional island of Kumani.

TABLE OF CONTENTS

Chapter One

THE FLAMES OF ANGER

The flames leaped high into the night air as sparks and embers shot off in every direction. The mob, highly agitated at their inability to penetrate the forest in pursuit of the dissenters, had returned to Oren's home to interrogate him further. When they discovered he was no longer there, rage took over. Within moments, the home where Oren and his family had spent so many wonderful years went up in flames.

Tanzi, the instigator of the whole event, stood off in the shadows quietly observing the fiery annihilation of the home in Zera. This was not the typical way the village elders handled those refusing to comply. Their ways were more subtle and less obvious to the ignorant folks managed and controlled by dictates of the elders. Now, this whole affair had grown into something that would cause the rabble to talk among themselves asking questions.

The flames danced in her eyes as the black-haired woman considered ways to turn the fury of the throng back to quiet submission. The village enforcers had allowed the passions of their anger to rise up against Oren for his lack of assistance in capturing his daughter, Shoshanna, the two escaped prisoners, Galen and Uri, along with her own son, Roany, now caught up in this rebellion. Tanzi would have to figure out a means to shift this whole burning mess to benefit both her plans and those of the village elders.

By the time the fire had slowly died, with only glowing embers remaining within the rubble of Oren's home, the woman had come up with a strategy. She needed to relay her new plan to the village elders for them to enact. With the crowd dispersing for the night, Tanzi became more determined than ever, to see this event quickly squelched so they could move forward with their plans.

Oren, having escaped the fury of the mob, wandered through the vegetation following a dim light appearing before him. With the fiery glow lighting up the night sky behind him, he knew he had nothing to return to at this point. Both his home and his past life were gone. There was nothing hindering him now as he pushed his way through the forest. Wherever this light was leading him, he was willing to go.

As he walked, he considered some of the things Shoshanna had shared with him prior to her escape into the woods. She spoke of a place somewhere on the island of Kumani where people lived and loved freely. He didn't even know what it was like to make decisions for himself. Throughout his entire life, he had been trained to follow village elders dictating their choices for the purpose of sustaining the existence of everyone on the island.

Now he was beginning to question it all.

It was quite late by the time the light led him to a quiet beach some distance from the smoldering ashes of his home. It vanished from sight as soon as he arrived. With the peaceful lapping waters of the sea and the shelter of the forest behind him, he could feel the tension melt off him as he relaxed. With no further plans or direction at the moment, he was quite content to set up camp at that location.

Though he had only some basic camping supplies collected after the mob left in pursuit of his daughter and her friends, it didn't take long for him to create a relatively comfortable site for him to sleep that night. With the smoky haze continuing its stagnant hold on the air around him, the shadowy form of the moon made its attempt to press through by dimly lighting the night skies.

A light breeze brushed over his weary face as his thinning hair stood at attention on the top of his head. Completing the task of making his bed, he decided it was too late for a fire. His stomach was still in knots over the many changes he had just experienced in a very short period of time. He had no idea what the future might hold for him.

The concept of having full control of his own life was foreign to Oren. It almost made him nervous as he realized he could go in any direction he chose. In truth, the light leading him brought a degree of comfort as he wasn't forced to immediately decide which way he needed to walk through the forest. Though he didn't understand the source of the light, somehow he retained a hope that possibly this mystery light might actually lead him to the "eagle lady" Shoshanna had spoken of in times past. He knew of no other person who might have the answers he needed.

Finally laying his head down on the pillow of blankets he had prepared, his mind ran through all the changes he had noticed in Shoshanna each time she returned from her "preparation time" with the eagle lady. Closing his eyes, Oren especially recalled the physical transformation he witnessed in his daughter after that first session with this woman. Her face glowed with new confidence and she radiated strength, and courage different from the timid child he had raised.

Maybe the eagle lady would have the same impact upon him. He hoped that somehow a new destiny and goal in life would materialize for him as well if only he could find this mysterious woman.

Eventually, all the trauma of the day faded from his mind as the lapping waters lulled him to sleep. His body was tired. Before long, only his gentle breathing could be heard as he drifted into the rest he desperately needed.

It was early the next morning when Oren finally awoke. As he opened his eyes, he was shocked to see a young girl standing on the beach beside him watching. Quickly, he sat up to get a better look at the child.

Smiling, the child greeted him. "Hi. I'm Jessah. Did you sleep well?"

Coughing to clear his throat, Oren grabbed his gourd and drank the water to moisten his dry throat before attempting to respond.

"Uh. Good morning. Yes, I slept well. I'm Oren."

"Hello, Oren," Jessah continued. "Are you hungry?"

"Well, actually I am quite hungry."

"Good!" she replied. "I'm here to invite you to come and enjoy a nice breakfast with us."

Oren's head was just beginning to clear up. He wasn't entirely sure if this was still a dream or reality.

"And who is this 'us' you speak of?" he asked.

"Miss Haddie and me. We would like you to come to join us for breakfast."

"Well, that does sound wonderful. If you will give me a moment to pack up, I'd be happy to follow you."

Jessah waited as Oren quickly rolled up his bedding and grabbed his supplies. Before long, the two of them were winding their way through the forest trails heading towards Miss Haddie's homestead.

Upon their arrival, Oren immediately noticed that the grounds surrounding the elegant cottage with flowering vines climbing up its sides were completely free of the normal haze surrounding every other area. Miss Haddie stepped out her front door, introduced herself, and warmly greeted their guest, as wafts of baked cinnamon and apples beckoned him in.

Once he entered her home, he noticed the table spread in preparation for breakfast. Fruit, muffins, apple turn-overs, and hot tea awaited him. With his rumpled clothing and unwashed face, he felt quite unprepared for such a feast, but at Miss Haddie's urging, he soon filled his very empty stomach.

With his hunger taken care of, Oren's mind was filled with a number of questions that were burning inside him. He didn't want to come across as too bold, so he held his tongue awaiting the right moment. However, before he even had a chance to ask, Miss Haddie answered him.

"Yes, I am the "eagle lady" Shoshanna spoke of," she said. "I was honored to have a part in training her these many weeks. She is a wonderful young woman. You have done an excellent job in raising her."

Oren smiled but was quick to redirect the praise. "Actually, it was my wife who deserves most of the credit for raising her. Dara died suddenly several years back and left me feeling quite helpless when it came to raising a daughter on my own."

Suddenly recalling the loss of his wife and the recent incineration of his home, he grew silent and introspective for a moment. It was apparent that everything he had worked so hard for his entire life had run through his fingers. Here he sat, a vagabond with no wife, no job, and no daughter to care for. He didn't even have a home to return to.

"Oren, let me assure you," Miss Haddie interrupted his thoughts. "You are not just a drifter, but with your recent choices, you have demonstrated you might be ready for a whole new life. I am here to help you discover that deeper destiny that was planted within you before you were ever born if you choose to do so."

"What is meant by a 'deeper destiny,'" Oren asked quite puzzled. His unspoken questions were answered a second time. "What does that actually mean?"

"Discovering your 'deeper destiny' is a part of learning who you really are and what you are capable of. The ability to hear real wisdom is the key to unlocking your destiny. In this gift you find the capacity to not only hear but to also discern the difference between truth and error. There is quite a history of this island that you are not yet aware of. Opposing forces have been at odds with each other for some time now."

Miss Haddie continued while peering deeply into his eyes.

"You have already witnessed the destructive powers of the one side, but I would like to introduce you to the source of light which led you here. Once you understand, who this is, you will be asked to make the choice on the type of life you want to live hereafter."

"If you think this is too much for you right now," she continued, "you will be asked to leave and may never see any of us again. Unfortunately, as you have already been identified as a dissenter, you will be forced to spend your days hiding and moving about in the forest to avoid being captured."

"If you choose to embrace this new life, you will be invited to remain here for a time in my guest cottage behind the house," Miss Haddie explained. "During this period, I will begin instructing you in the ways of the eagle, just as I did with Shoshanna. She chose for herself and now you will be given the same opportunity. Is this clear?"

"Yes, very clear," Oren responded.

"Very well. Jessah will escort you out to the cottage where you may set up and rest for a time before lunch. After lunch, we will begin our history lesson."

Once Miss Haddie was done, she stood up from the table and gathered up the dishes. Jessah, who had been sitting quietly listening to the speech, also stood up.

"Come, Oren," she invited him. "I will show you where the guest cottage is so you can put your things away."

Solemnly, Oren stood and followed the young girl out the back door. A stone footpath led the way to a small cottage with a fire burning in the fireplace and a lamp lit to provide adequate lighting. Once there, Jessah took a step back allowing the man to enter for himself.

He took a quick glance around and nodded to the child indicating that the accommodations were adequate. Once he was inside, Jessah skipped back on the footpath reentering the home with Miss Haddie.

Oren certainly had a lot to consider as he unpacked putting his meager camping supplies off to the side of the room. He knew this afternoon was key to him finally having some of his questions answered, but also realized that more questions would undoubtedly arise. For now, he had to accept his precarious position as a temporary guest with an unknown future.

Chapter Two

A NEW DAY

It was already daylight when Shoshanna awakened. While stretching, she wiped the sleep out of her hazel eyes. Glancing around, she realized she was inside a tent. It took a few moments before the events of the previous day flooded in.

Oh yes! She recalled her early morning journey to inform Miss Haddie of the shortened time the village elders had given her to prepare for a forced marriage to whomever they chose. Once there, the young girl, Jessah arrived and the three of them prepared food while they visited.

Later that afternoon, Galen and his two friends showed up, apparently on the run and heading for the smoking mountains. After their meal together, they were all surprised by Miss Haddie's announcement that Shoshanna was to join them on their journey.

After their departure from Miss Haddie's homestead, the foursome traveled first to Shoshanna's home in Zera so she could say goodbye to her father. After that, they planned to continue towards the discovery of the Eagles' Nest where they would apparently be safe. While saying her final farewells, the village enforcers showed up causing the group to flee into the forest.

Somehow they all had avoided capture and were met by their new friend, Chen from the Eagles' Nest. He directed them to a prepared campsite surrounded by the forest. They watched in awe as the trees and foliage grew in around them creating a safe environment for them to sleep for the night.

Shoshanna's heart raced even as she thought about the previous day. Would they still be locked in by the trees, she wondered as she pulled back the flap of her tent.

The moment she looked out, she realized the surrounding trees and foliage had returned to their normal size. A fire was already burning in the center of their tents and spread upon a blanket set upon the ground was a meal all ready for them to enjoy. While she was still studying the outdoors from the safety of her tent, Galen stepped out of the trees carrying a few more pieces of wood to add to the fire.

Relieved to see her friend already up and moving, Shoshanna scrambled out of her blankets and joined him as he threw the broken branches into the fire.

"How did you sleep?" he inquired as she stepped closer to the flames.

"I slept wonderfully. I guess I really was tired from all the commotion yesterday," she admitted. Galen nodded. He definitely understood, so Shoshanna continued. "So, I need to ask you. Did we really see these trees grow around us last night?"

"Yes, we did."

"And did we see Chen step through them as if they were not there?" she continued.

"We saw that as well."

"Can you explain that please? I have never seen anything like that before." Galen looked over in her direction before speaking.

"Honestly, I have never seen anything like that myself, though you do recall seeing the foliage cover Miss Haddie's homestead before. Right?"

Shoshanna nodded as Galen continued. "All I can say is that this must be a new level of that same type of manifestation. I suspect we will be seeing a lot more of that as the light leads us closer to the Eagles' Nest." Galen paused for a moment before adding another thought on this topic.

"I think this journey is all about us being further prepared as we face the challenges that Chen indicated we would encounter."

"What kind of challenges do you think we might face?" she asked.

"I'm not really sure, but I suspect there may be physical as well as mental challenges we will need to overcome."

Just as Galen was finishing his speculations on the journey before them, both Roany and Uri came out of their tents joining them around the fire.

"What was that I heard about challenges we need to overcome?" Roany responded. "After all that we have already gone through, I'm pretty sure that we will be able to make it through whatever the smoking mountains decide to throw our way." Uri had to agree.

"I'm not worried about any physical challenges," he added confidently as he patted his muscular biceps. "I think I got that covered."

"Remember what Chen said?" Galen reminded them. "He said this journey would test our endurance. He also told us to not let peripheral things distract us. He mentioned fear and our imaginations as important things we needed to conquer. To me, this sounds like it might involve the things we allow to consume our thoughts. That sounds a lot tougher than just muscling our way through things, doesn't it?"

"Yeah, it does," Roany admitted.

Galen continued. "I suggest we take the warnings of Chen very seriously, especially since we don't know what lies ahead in the smoking mountains."

Just hearing all the discussions of what Chen had already told them, Shoshanna started feeling even more nervous about the journey. She wondered if she might be the weak link as they battled their way to the Eagles' Nest.

"I only learned I was to go on this journey with you at Miss Haddie's," Shoshanna interjected. "What if I can't press through all the challenges?"

Galen had to smile. "You know, most likely, we are all thinking the same thing. What gives me the confidence to even attempt this journey is the fact that Elemet sent Chen to direct all four of us to do this together. Miss Haddie confirmed this as well at her homestead. There *are* to be four of us on this adventure. Knowing this, I am confident that each of us will discover new areas of strength we had not been aware of previously as we progress through the mountains. Don't you agree?"

"Yes, you are right, Galen," Roany responded. "Our confidence cannot be based on what we think are our strengths, but we can be confident in that Elemet believes we are strong enough to do this."

With all their concerns about the journey temporarily laid aside, the four young adults sat down around the fire to enjoy their last meal before stepping into whatever lay ahead of them in the smoking mountains. Once the meal was completed, the group quickly packed up the remaining food, loaded up their knapsacks, and after extinguishing the fire, they started their journey through the unknown regions towards the Eagles' Nest.

Chapter Three

A "HELPING" HAND

As Giza poured some steaming water into her cup, a hard knock at the front door startled her causing some water to spill. Her heart was still pounding so she paused momentarily before answering the door. With all the activity of the last several months, she certainly had noticed an increase of visitors, far beyond the occasional social call of her good friend, Adina.

Opening the door, she was surprised to see an unfamiliar young man standing with a freshly prepared chicken in his hand and a smile upon his face. With his wavy chestnut brown hair, though lighter than Galen's hair, he was nearly a replica of their missing son.

"Hi. My name is Mendi. I live on the other side of Kieran and heard a little about the unfortunate events involving your son, Galen. And let me say, I am so sorry about your difficulties. As I thought about it, it occurred to me that maybe you and your husband might be in need of some assistance from time to time. I had this extra chicken at home and wondered if you might be able to use it?" he asked.

Giza stood astonished, unable to respond momentarily. "Oh, excuse me," she said apologetically. "I was just taken back a little at how much you look like our son. What was I thinking? Please come in." Taking the chicken, she gratefully set it near her sink and washed her hands, before continuing.

"Would you like some tea to drink? I was just preparing some for myself."

"That would be great," Mendi replied. "You know, I am a handy guy as well and am willing to come and help both you and your husband occasionally."

"Oh, that is so kind of you!" she responded. Pouring the remainder of the hot water into a second cup, she returned with the two cups of tea and set them at the table, motioning for Mendi to sit down and join her. "Let me call my husband, Eber in so he can meet you as well. He's just working outside."

"Of course."

As Mendi sat down, Giza rushed outside to the spot where Eber had been working.

A little breathless, she called over to her husband as he lifted the ax to split another log. With perspiration beading upon his forehead, he looked up.

"Eber! We have a guest." she blurted out. "You need to come to meet this young man. Wait until you see him. Besides having lighter colored hair, he resembles our son so much!"

Silently, Eber stared at Giza with his cold blue eyes before responding. "We have no son."

Tears welled up in Giza's eyes at such harsh words. She knew their son, Galen was only doing what he felt was right and she would never reject him for following his conscience in this matter. However, in spite of her husband's foul mood, she was determined to at least have him meet this young man.

"He has brought us a fine cooked chicken and says he wants to help us around the house from time to time. I really think you need to come in and meet him."

Still annoyed at this disruption, Eber reluctantly agreed to come inside briefly to greet their visitor. Wiping the sweat from his face with a handkerchief, he laid down the ax and followed his wife into the cabin.

As soon as they entered, Mendi quickly stood and extended his hand to the silvery-haired man approaching him.

"Hello sir," the young man said. "I am Mendi. So happy to meet you. I was just telling your wife that I don't live too far and would be happy to help you with chores or projects around the house you may need some assistance with."

Shaking his hand, Eber briefly sized up the man standing before him. "That is mighty kind of you, but I think I can handle things for now."

"Are you sure? I am a carpenter by trade and am pretty handy with the hammer," Mendi encouraged them.

"What about the difficulties you had trying to repair the roof recently?" Giza reminded her husband. "Couldn't Mendi help with that?"

At first, Eber was slightly irritated with his wife mentioning his troubles before others, but noticing the hopefulness in his wife's soft brown eyes, he had to concede. He did need some help.

"Alright, Mendi. I guess I could use some help around this place once in a while. She also tells me you brought us a chicken. Thank you."

"Oh, you are very welcome! When would you like me to come and help you with that roof?"

"I guess we could try tackling that tomorrow if you have the time," Eber suggested.

"I could do that," Mendi responded. "As a carpenter, I have lots of flexibility with my time. Would you like me to come after breakfast tomorrow?"

"Oh, no!" Giza interrupted. "Please join us for breakfast, if you are able."

"Well, thank you, ma'am!" he smiled. "That is mighty kind of you. I would love to join you for breakfast."

"Okay, then it is settled," Giza declared. "We will see you for breakfast tomorrow."

"Perfect," he replied, "I do need to head back into town right now. I have a few things to attend to so I can be free tomorrow. Thank you for the tea, Giza. Is it alright if I call you that?"

"Of course! And you can call my husband, Eber," she said with a smile.

"Wonderful to meet you, Giza and Eber. I am looking forward to both breakfast and working together on your roof," he responded while heading towards the door.

"Thank you, young man," Eber replied with just a hint of a smile finally emerging.

The elderly couple watched from their door as Mendi headed out back towards Kieran. Once his back was turned to the couple, he couldn't help but smile at his own skill in so quickly winning the old couple over to him.

Wait until I tell Tanzi and the village elders about this new friendship, he smugly thought to himself. They will certainly be impressed with how quickly I work!

The young man hurried off to report his progress to those awaiting the details of his encounter.

Chapter Four

ALL HANDS ON DECK

With a woven basket hanging over her arm, Yona pressed through the unusually large crowd of people gathering in the center of their village. She was only interested in one thing; the necessary purchase of fresh fruit and vegetables she had been sent to get for Ms. Bina. Though only twelve years old, with her flowing brown hair and stunning dark eyes, Yona appeared much older and could easily pass for a young woman in her late teens.

As she passed by a group of young men standing together, they couldn't help but notice this new addition to their village of Chana. Focused only on the market located on the other side of the street, Yona gazed downward so as to avoid eye contact with any of the gawkers. Mercifully, their inspection was interrupted by a public announcement in the center of the marketplace.

"Good people of Chana, I have been sent here to speak on behalf of the elders from some of the surrounding villages to ask for your help," the young man said, standing on top of a wooden crate turned upside down as a stage. "Several of our villages have been plagued by a group of escaped dissenters who have fled into the woods out of our reach. These dangerous individuals have already burned one home to the ground and are looking to cause havoc in other locations as well."

Conversations rippled through the crowd as Yona stopped in her tracks and turned to hear what other propaganda this man had to promote. Though she had not heard much about Jessah's exploits, she hoped her friend had used wisdom to avoid being labeled a dissenter.

Memories of the many "lessons" she had been taught at the orphanage or "Camp Shabelle" where both she and Jessah lived for many years before she was sent to work for Ms. Bina as a household maid. Fortunately, the move had been a good one for her as Ms. Bina, though blind, was very kind, even treating Yona as a granddaughter rather than just a maid. She wasn't sure if Jessah was still at Camp Shabelle, but she did know that if someone caught her escaping as she did from the confines of the retraining center, her friend would be in great trouble.

"The village elders have decided to release sketches of the escaped dissenters in hopes that if you happen to see any of them in your midst, you could quickly report this to the elders. These sketches will be posted outside of the village gathering place for all of you to see." The man continued.

"We are also looking for some strong young men who would be willing to help us comb the forest regions around us, even leading up to the smoking mountains so that we might recapture these rebels before anything else happens. A generous bounty has been placed on each of their heads, should any of you assist us in their capture. Do I have any volunteers?" he asked.

Immediately, the hands of the recent gawkers shot up and the young man on the crate called them over along with other volunteers for further instructions. Many of the men assembled together around the messenger, eager for the promised bounties.

Yona shook her head in disgust as she watched the gathering dupes enthusiastically volunteering for the man-hunt while she moved in another direction. Nervously, she forced her way through the crowd until she was able to look at the posted drawings of the escaped dissenters with their names listed below.

Relieved, she saw that Jessah's name was not on the list. Though her friend was only ten years old, she knew that any contact she had with dissenters could be devastating for her. Memorizing the names and faces of those they were looking for, Yona quickly turned to finish her shopping before Ms. Bina became concerned.

After shopping, Yona hurried back to the house. Once the food was properly stored, she found a piece of parchment and quickly wrote out the names she had seen listed as dissenters. Jessah would need to know this the next time she visited.

It wasn't long before Ms. Bina was calling for her beloved companion to sit with her so they could visit. Yona debated whether or not she should inform the elderly woman of what she had seen and heard that afternoon in the marketplace. Sooner or later, Ms. Bina would certainly ask about activities in the village. For now, Yona decided to wait until she could better plan out what to say and what information to withhold.

It was quite late in the afternoon by the time Oren had finished his history lesson with Miss Haddie. Much like his daughter, he felt enraged at all the shenanigans happening behind closed doors without the knowledge of villagers across the island. Once he came to understand exactly what the "way of the eagle" referred to, he was ready that moment to join this call for true freedom coming from Elemet himself.

As always, Miss Haddie encouraged her student to take some time to fully consider the effects his choice would mean upon his life before proceeding ahead. However, given his current circumstances, which his teacher had so clearly laid out for him, he really didn't see any other decision he could make. Shoshanna was already in and now, so was he.

Realizing that Oren had already made some important decisions by following the light the night before, Miss Haddie agreed that they could continue with his training. With only short breaks for meals, the teacher taught, and the student eagerly drank in truth with an insatiable thirst. He was ready!

Even while focusing on her lessons, Miss Haddie could sense something dark preparing traps for those living on the island as a part of their devious plans to keep everything as it had been. She realized that Oren's intense training was designed for his own protection once he left the safety of her homestead.

Though only ten, Jessah would need to learn a new way of moving around the island as well. Her days of traveling freely through the forests were coming to an end. Now was the time for the next wave of gifting and wisdom to be unleashed upon those already moving in the way of the eagle. Miss Haddie could sense it.

With this new level of gifting and wisdom came a higher intensity of persecution as well. No longer would there be much room for error for those following the light. Either they followed instructions exactly, or severe consequences would follow. This was not a time to take things lightly!

Chapter Five

MAKING PROGRESS

With their campsite now far behind them, Galen, Uri, Roany, and Shoshanna pressed forward through the rough, volcanic-like rocks found all over the smoking mountains. Each step had to be carefully placed or one could easily twist an ankle if the rocks happen to move in the wrong direction. In addition to the hazardous footing, the smoke seemed much denser than before causing their visibility to be greatly diminished.

Galen was leading the group by following the light barely visible before him. There was little conversation taking place as it took all their energy to avoid stumbling as they put one foot in front of each other. Though the tired travelers were not speaking, each had a number of thoughts whirling around in their heads adding to the stress. Roany got to the point when he just couldn't handle it any longer!

"That's it!" he announced. "I'm done. I can't press through this mess with all these crazy thoughts running around in my head. Is anyone else having a problem like me?"

Galen and the others stopped, actually relieved to sit for a moment and take a break. Once he caught his breath, Galen responded. "No Roany. You are not the only one fighting thoughts. I have been hearing voices telling me to quit and give up ever since we started. I agree. It is exhausting!" The other two also admitted to battling mental attacks as well.

"Is there anything we can do to eliminate these distractions?" Shoshanna asked.

"I'm not sure," Galen admitted. "Why don't we each take a moment to quiet ourselves so we can receive some wisdom on what to do?"

"I don't know," Uri commented. "I'm not too good at hearing yet. Maybe it would be better for me to just follow whatever you decide."

"Uri, don't make the mistake of putting all your trust in us," Galen encouraged him. "The time may come when we will not be around, and you will need to hear for yourself. I know that is what Elemet wants. We are all learning how to hear and follow directions better. Besides, the only way we can get better is by using the little we have. Once, we are faithful with that, we are given more."

Shoshanna also spoke up. "You know, I am still very new at all this. I definitely did not feel ready for a journey of this magnitude, but obviously, Elemet sees within each of us the ability to overcome this. You were invited on this journey and I'm sure you can finish it with all of us."

Suddenly Roany, grabbing his head, cried out in pain.

"I feel like my head is going to explode! You guys need to do something fast!" he cried out.

Quickly, the others gathered around Roany and listened so they would know how to help their friend. For a few moments, the group was silent as they waited for instructions, even as Roany groaned in pain.

Looking up, Shoshanna looked at her friend with her eyes squinted. "I see a gray cloud swirling around his head. Galen, what is that?" No sooner had Shoshanna asked the question, when some insight entered Galen's mind.

"Roany, I know you said you wanted to explore this new lifestyle with us, but have you asked Elemet himself to direct your life?"

With his hands still gripping his head in pain, Roany admitted he had never done that before.

"I think it's time for you to ask him yourself. There is no way we can complete this journey on our own," Galen advised him.

"Okay, okay. I'm ready to ask for help," Roany replied. With his eyes closed, the young man made his appeal to Elemet, admitting that he no longer desired to direct his own life any further. He asked for help and the assistance he needed to continue the journey before them.

As they all watched, a light, clearly visible in the smoke, swirled around Roany's head in the opposite direction of the gray cloud Shoshanna had seen earlier. As the light encircled his head, the pressure Roany was feeling decreased with each passing moment until finally, the gray cloud completely vanished from sight. As the gray cloud disappeared, so did the pressure Roany was feeling.

Uri, amazed at what had just happened, had many questions. Galen did his best to answer them all one by one until finally, Galen postponed the discussion so they could focus on the pressing journey before them. Just as they were ready to move on, Shoshanna spoke up excitedly.

"Look at that stone Roany is sitting on! There's something on it."

Once Roany stood so the others could better examine the stone, they all noticed the chiseled outline of an eagle with outspread wings clearly portrayed. Each of them took turns examining the eagle close up. A renewed hope and endurance seemed to rise up as they recalled Chen's description of the markers they were to watch for along the way. With new confidence arising in each of them, the onslaught of negative thoughts gradually decreased, granting them the break they so desperately needed.

Though the afternoon sun was beginning to sink closer to the horizon, the four friends decided to press on a little further before stopping for the night. As they moved along the trail, Shoshanna worked her way up to Galen's side. She needed to ask him something.

"I need to know. What exactly was that gray cloud I saw whirling around Roany's head? It appeared to be almost alive as it attacked Roany."

"It is alive," Galen responded. "Do you remember our discussion when I was taking you back to your village? We spoke about darkness attempting to enslave us by getting us to agree with its lies. Remember?"

Shoshanna nodded as Galen continued.

"Roany believed the lie that it was not necessary for him to completely yield to Elemet and his light. He thought that if he just hung out with the rest of us, he would be fine. But that is not the case, as you just witnessed."

"Though we were each being bombarded by lies, Roany had no power to resist the attack until he fully yielded himself to Elemet and his plans," Galen explained. "What you saw was a battle between darkness and light. However, we know that light obviously won," he added with a smile.

"Will we ever get to the place where our thoughts will not be assaulted anymore?" Shoshanna asked.

"I don't know if we will be free and clear on this portion of our journey," he responded. "I have a feeling that this hike through the haze was designed to reveal any lies that we may yet be agreeing with. Our agreement empowers darkness to attack at will. However, once a lie is identified and removed, the light is able to come in and defeat the darkness."

Shoshanna grew silent for a moment before speaking.

"I'm nervous about that."

"Why?"

"What if there is some lie I believe that is going to show up and throw me off a cliff or something?" she asked, looking downward. Feeling a little ashamed about such a silly question, she explained, "I had a dream about that once and as I heard those lying voices speaking, something pushed me off a cliff. I had no power to stop them."

"Was that dream before or after you met Elemet?" he probed.

"Before I met Elemet."

"See, you didn't have the power you needed to stop the voices at the time of your dream. However, things have changed quite a bit since you met Elemet, haven't they?"

"Oh, yes!"

"You actually do have the power to overcome now," he continued. "All darkness can do at this point is try to get you to agree with fear. It wants you to feel afraid and powerless, though the opposite is true. We cannot allow what we feel to dictate what we do. We must only be moved by what we know is true. Understand?"

"I think so," Shoshanna replied. "So how can I battle these crazy feelings?"

Smiling, Galen continued. "I have learned rather than trying not to think about fear, it seems to work best if I focus on what is good, pure, and true in my life. Once I look at those things, I feel thankful and encouraged rather than the opposite. Thankfulness is a powerful weapon against the enemy of fear."

Shoshanna studied Galen's face momentarily as he confidently followed the light before him.

"And what are you thankful for?" she asked him with a twinkle in her eye.

"Right now, I am thankful for a friend like you who reminds me to be thankful at all times," he replied with a grin.

Shoshanna laughed and then one second later, she screamed out a warning to the others.

Posed behind a large boulder ahead of them were two men from the villages who had been looking for the escaped dissenters. Jumping out from behind their hiding place, the men laughed as they blocked the passage of the travelers while swinging their heavy chains and axes threatening the group. Turning back to retreat, the group found another man, equally armed, ready to prevent their escape as well.

Recognizing that they were surrounded, Galen looked upward cried out.

"Elemet!"

The moment his name was spoken, a blinding light surrounded each of the three attackers causing them to fall to the ground as they cried out in shock.

"Where did they go? I can't see where I'm going!" one of them called out to the other two. The others complained of the same thing as they felt around for the weapons they had dropped.

Motioning to his friends to remain silent, Galen led them around the two men scrambling on the ground, searching in confusion. Once they passed their attackers, they doubled their pace to make certain there was a good distance between them and the enforcers.

When they felt safe again, Shoshanna spoke up.

"I didn't think those enforcers could find us here in the smoking mountains! I always thought the villagers were too afraid to enter these regions."

"I'll bet they put a bounty on our heads," Roany suggested. "That's the only thing I know of that would cause people to willingly travel up here."

"You are probably right," Galen agreed. "Well, that changes things for us. Now that we know they are looking for us in the smoking mountains as well, we will need to be much more vigilant, that is for sure. Hopefully, it will be a while before they are able to report our location to the village elders."

"There are plenty of stones here. We could use them to defend ourselves," Uri volunteered.

Laughing to himself, Galen looked back at his burly, redheaded friend. "Yes, I guess we could throw a few rocks at them, but you have to admit, Elemet's way seemed a lot more efficient to me, didn't it?"

Uri smiled in agreement. "Yeah. That was pretty good. Where did that blinding light come from anyway?"

"Didn't you hear me call out his name?" Galen asked.

"Yeah."

"So, we just saw that the same light directing us will also protect us. Good to know, right?"

"Oh yeah! That is good to know," Uri replied.

"I'm sure we will be learning quite a bit more about all this as we continue," Galen concluded.

With all the excitement behind them, the group continued their trek at a steady pace, but always on the alert as they scanned the regions they were traveling through. Weariness set in as the sun touched the distant horizon, but still, they pressed forward until a suitable location could be found for them to rest that evening.

Just as Shoshanna was beginning to feel she had no more to give, they spotted a cave which appeared to be safe enough. They were taking no chances, so the men decided to scout out the region a little before setting up. Exhausted, Shoshanna decided to sit on a boulder close to the cave entrance while waiting for the others to return.

Leaning back against the side of the cave, her fingers touched upon an uneven surface that felt a little different. Some of the branches of a rough bramble covered the region, but pulling the branch off to the side, Shoshanna saw something that brought a sense of great relief to her.

"Galen! Roany! Uri!" she called out. "Come see what I have found!"

The three men quickly returned to the cave entrance. As they watched, Shoshanna pulled back the branch revealing an eagle carved into the stone. The carving gave them the assurance they needed that this was a safe location. As night set in, the foursome entered the cave and quickly set up their campsite.

The men were a little disappointed that there was no fire already burning, nor prepared meal awaiting them as it had been before, but Shoshanna assured them they still had plenty of food remaining in their knapsacks to satisfy their hunger. Uri wasn't sure there was enough food for him alone, much less for everyone else, but still agreed to equally divide up what they had.

While the men went out to gather wood for the fire, Shoshanna took the lead in proportioning the food between them. By the time the fire blazed heating the cave to a comfortable level, their meager rations were placed on cloth napkins for each of them to enjoy. Uri, however, was not impressed at all! His food looked no larger than what he considered a mere snack. Realizing he had no other choice at the moment, he decided to eat what he had without complaining.

Roany was the first to notice something different about the food. As they ate, the amount of food did not seem to diminish, but rather stayed the same, that is until they found themselves full and quite content.

Once Roany pointed that out, they had to marvel at the varying methods Elemet demonstrated in his care for them. With full bellies and a warm spot to sleep, each of them found a comfortable spot in the cave, rolled up in their own blankets, and using their knapsacks as pillows for their heads, they each fell into a peaceful sleep rather quickly.

However, even as the others rested, Galen's mind drifted into a place where he clearly saw his parents at their home in Kieran. Though they appeared well enough, he sensed a warning arise in his soul. Encroaching darkness was in play threatening their safety. He had no idea what that might be, but his growing uneasiness caused him to call out to the only name he knew for help in this matter.

Something was definitely amiss.

Chapter Six

THE WAY OF THE EAGLE

Several days had passed since Oren had begun his intense training in the way of the eagle. Miss Haddie led the instruction, but Jessah eagerly shared her own experiences as well to help Oren better understand this new way of living. As a climax to her dramatic narrative describing the night Elemet took her flying on the back of a golden eagle, she proudly produced the large feather with its gold streaks running through it.

Oren was speechless at first as he examined the feather close up.

"You found this in your bed, you say?" he asked.

"Yes! I woke up after flying all over the island. This feather was right beside me."

Oren shook his head in amazement as he turned the plume round and round between his fingers.

"Well, this certainly demonstrates the reality of what you experienced," he commented. "Makes me wonder what other new things might be revealed as we move ahead.

Obviously, there's much more to discover in the ways of the eagle."

Miss Haddie smiled as she observed the progress of her new student. Allowing him time to reflect, she turned her attention to Jessah.

"So, my dear, I've been thinking about how confining this place must feel to you at times."

"Oh no! This is not confining at all! I love it here and love being with you as well!" Jessah exclaimed.

"Well, you do remember that I am in need of someone to deliver messages for me from time to time. Right?"

"Yes, I remember."

"Elemet has been talking to me about someone very dear to me; Ms. Bina. I think it might be time for me to send her a greeting. Don't you think that is a great idea?"

"Does that mean I get to spend time with Yona as well?" Jessah asked excitedly.

"I am sure that will happen as well, however, we do need to discuss how you are to get back and forth from their home in Chana. Many more dangers have arisen in recent days that would make it difficult for you to travel through the forests as you have before."

Jessah listened attentively with her eyes wide open in anticipation.

"Elemet has sent you a new mode of transportation that I think you will find enjoyable. Why don't we all step out the back door so we can see what he has prepared."

Miss Haddie led the way with both Oren and Jessah close behind. When she opened the back door, both of them gasped in surprise. Standing in the back portion of her homestead was a huge golden eagle gently flapping his wings in excited expectation.

"It's him! It's him!" Jessah cried out in delight. Without a moment's hesitation, the child ran out the door grabbing the eagle's neck in a warm embrace. As they watched, one wing softly wrapped around the young girl, giving what appeared to be an embrace.

Once again, Oren was without words as he saw for himself the magnificent creature Jessah had only recently described to him. Miss Haddie followed the child outside and motioned for Oren to join them as they stood alongside the eagle with its shimmering golden feathers.

Jessah called her friends closer to the eagle allowing them to admire his intense eyes, sharp beak, and lethal-looking talons. The gilded highlights of his feathers reflected the bright rays of the sun creating brilliant flashes of light around him. This massive bird was not to be trifled with for sure.

After examining the incredible animal, Miss Haddie continued.

"Now child, you have already had some experience in riding this great bird, but you must remember that he is on a mission, just like you are. He has been directed only to take you to Ms. Bina's home and then to bring you back when you are finished."

"How will he know when I am done?" she asked.

"Oh, he will know! He's great friends with Elemet. Remember?"

"Yes, I remember," Jessah responded.

"So are you ready to go flying and send my greetings to Ms. Bina?"

"I am so ready!"

"Well then, climb aboard, child. Your escort is waiting."

Giggling in utter delight, Jessah stepped up beside the bird's great wing. The eagle's outspread wing allowed her to climb up and straddle his body. Grabbing hold of his neck feathers, the girl flattened her body next to his. Once she was in position, the bird flapped his wings and easily rose into the air. Jessah quickly waved as she flew through the skies out on her mission.

Oren's mouth was still gaping as he watched both the child and the eagle glide out of sight. Miss Haddie had already turned back towards the cottage when she called out behind her.

"Come along, Oren. We still need to discuss your new method of travel as well so you can be prepared when you are sent out on your first mission."

This statement caught his attention and curiosity. Quickly, he spun around and headed inside so he could hear what Miss Haddie had to say.

Meanwhile, Jessah took in every moment of her exhilarating flight as they pressed through the haze into the brilliantly blue skies above them. Once the eagle ended his ascent, Jessah was able to gaze down upon the island below as she searched for familiar landmarks that would indicate where they might be.

Though she knew the haze blocked their view while on the ground, her overview of the landscape was unhindered while in the atmosphere above. The first place she recognized was the village of Zera where both Oren and his daughter, Shoshanna had lived. On the outskirts of the village, she could clearly see burnt ruins of a cabin that obviously once belonged to Oren. Only ashes remained, just as he suspected.

Next, Jessah identified the village of Kieran where both Galen and Roany had come from. Located in a rolling meadow, she easily identified Galen's home. She even spotted his parents standing outside as a young man she did not recognize was working on their roof. Something about that disturbed her a little, though she didn't know why.

The eagle continued on his way until he approached a grove of trees with a clearing close by. Protected by the trees, the eagle landed safely. Jessah knew it was time for her to slip off and follow the light leading her in the direction she needed. As she was taken in close proximity to where she needed to go, she soon arrived in the village of Chana.

Jessah quietly moved among the trees approaching the back door of Ms. Bina's cabin. After knocking, she waited until Yona responded and opened the door for her friend. The two immediately embraced. Afterwards Jessah explained the purpose of her visit.

Once they realized Ms. Bina was a friend of Miss Haddie's, there was no longer any worry about her meeting Jessah. Yona brought her friend in and introduced her to

Ms. Bina. The visit blossomed into a lively discussion of all that had transpired since Jessah's move to Miss Haddie's homestead.

There was much each of them needed to share.

Chapter Seven

TRAINING INTENSIVE

"**N**o, keep your eyes closed!" Miss Haddie instructed.

"But how am I supposed to see where I am going?" Oren complained.

"You don't need to see with your natural eyes until you can perceive what is actually around you," she insisted. "Now, what are you sensing?"

Taking a breath, he found himself feeling a little frustrated with her ambitious attempts to push him into this new way of living. Again, Oren tried focusing on things beyond what his natural eyes could grasp.

"I don't see anything," he grumbled, but no sooner had he spoken than his closed eyes detected something he had never seen before. "Wait. I do see something," he corrected himself.

"Good! Tell me what you are seeing," she encouraged him.

"It's like a pulsating blue light right in your direction."

"Okay, now I am going to move around the room and I want you to follow the light you see."

Oren, still with his eyes closed, accurately followed his teacher about the room without stumbling over any of the furniture she negotiated around.

"Wonderful! Now you can open your eyes."

"So what was that?" he asked, clearly puzzled.

"That was seeing the reality of the life I live in. Everyone who has come into agreement with Elemet has this very same light emanating around them as well, just as you do."

"Really?"

"Yes! This is one way in which you will be able to discern who is dwelling in truth and who is still remaining in the shadows of confusion. There is also another wonderful gift you have been given that I would like to help you develop," Miss Haddie continued.

"And what is that?"

"Do you remember that thorny hedge which grew around your cabin when the enforcers were attempting to capture your daughter and the others?"

"Yes," he responded. He clearly recalled the thick hedge as it grew up suddenly protecting the four young adults as they hurried off into the forest. As the pursuing enforcers attempted to chop down the hedge, it only grew thicker and denser.

"Now, when you decided you needed to also escape into the forest, what happened when you stepped into the hedge?" she prodded him.

"I closed my eyes, stepped into it, and when I opened my eyes, I was in the forest on the other side of the hedge."

"Exactly! That is a gift Elemet wants to further develop within you as well."

"So, how does that work?" Oren asked, intrigued by her statement.

Rather than trying to explain the gift further, Miss Haddie invited Oren to follow her outside as she led him into the forested area just beyond the perimeter of her homestead.

"Now, I want you to stand in front of this tree and close your eyes once again."

Oren stepped up placing his face next to the large tree trunk closing his eyes as instructed.

"So, in moments when you are in danger of detection from those who may be pursuing or even coming near you, you will be able to use this gift to step into and out of things that appear impenetrable. Are you ready to try?"

"Wait! What are you telling me to do?"

"With your eyes closed, I want you to step into that tree, wait a moment, and then step out on the other side of it."

Turning back to look at Miss Haddie, Oren asked again, "Go through a tree? Are you sure?"

"Close your eyes again and focus. Don't look at me!" she corrected her student.

Taking a breath, a little uneasy about this wild directive, Oren once again closed eyes and focused.

"What do you see?" she asked once again.

Oren waited until something became clear before him. As he stared at the back of his eyelids, he noticed an object slowly coming into focus.

"Ok. I see something!" he exclaimed. "I see a doorway in front of me."

"Wonderful! Now, with your eyes still closed, I want you to step into it and tell me what happens when you do that."

Taking a step forward, instead of running into the tree, Oren stepped into the doorway before him. As Miss Haddie watched, he disappeared from her sight.

"Oren, now tell me what is happening."

"It's hard to describe! So beautiful here with clouds and colors swirling all around me!" he called out from his hidden location.

"Okay, now take another step forward with your eyes still shut." Obediently, Oren took another step forward appearing on the opposite side of the tree. Flabbergasted at what had just occurred, he quickly stepped back around the tree to face Miss Haddie once again.

"What was that?"

"You have been given the ability to step into another realm whenever others are pursuing you," she explained. "This will not work all the time, but only when you see a door for you to step into when your eyes are shut. This is just another of the many tools you have been given as you enter into the adventure you were designed for on the island of Kumani."

Turning back towards her homestead, Miss Haddie continued. "So now that you understand this gift, let us go back inside where we can discuss some of the strategies Elemet has planned for this new season of your life."

As they walked into the cottage, Oren had to look back one more time at the tree he had just passed through, still shaking his head in amazement. He could not even imagine what other surprises Elemet had for him in the days ahead.

Chapter Eight

PERIPHERAL THINGS

Galen woke up with a start thinking of parents he had left behind in his home village of Kieran. The nagging idea that they might be in danger persisted even as he got up and prepared to venture out in search of firewood and something to offer his companions for breakfast.

As he climbed to the top of the knoll directly above the cave where the others were still sleeping, he noticed a lone apple tree growing with numerous ripe apples hanging from its branches. Eagerly, Galen moved towards the tree pulling out his shirt to drop the apples into so he could bring them to his companions.

While focusing on reaching the nearby apples, he suddenly heard a deep-throated growl reverberate from behind him causing the very hair on his arms to stand up on edge. Slowly turning around, Galen found himself surrounded by a pack of wolves hungrily staring at their new discovery. With a heart pounding inside his chest, his first thought was to hurl the apples at his adversaries, but he doubted that would be very effective and would probably result in aggravating them further.

He continued staring at the snarling creatures while slowly backing up, but before he got too far, he realized the pack had split up and surrounded him. Running away was not an option and calling for assistance from his friends was pointless as he realized they were still sleeping deep in the cave. They would hear nothing.

Struggling to find the peace and clarity he was accustomed to, Galen silently cried out to Elemet, asking for both the wisdom and deliverance he needed at that moment. There were no other options.

Turning to keep his attention on all the wolves which were obviously preparing to attack, he watched as the circle they created around their victim grew smaller and smaller. Galen, realizing there was no apparent way of escape, decided to close his eyes, fully expecting sharp teeth and claws to penetrate any moment. As he stood his ground, he suddenly realized the growling and snarling had ceased.

Opening his eyes to see what had happened and rather than a pack of snarling wolves, he saw a face that brought him great relief and joy.

"Chen!" he exclaimed. "I thought I was going to be breakfast for some hungry wolves. I'm so glad to see you!"

"You asked for assistance, right?"

"Oh yes, I definitely did," Galen replied, still in a sweat.

Chen encouraged the young man to follow him to the other side of the knoll where a dancing fire crackled beckoning him to sit upon the fallen logs carefully placed around it. Hot mugs of steaming tea awaited them along with a lavish array of breakfast foods already prepared.

Walking up to the feast, Galen almost felt ashamed at the few apples he had managed to collect for his hungry friends back in the cave. He realized that the whole morning had been designed to teach him something new. Piling the apples on the ground next to him, he sat down on the log across from Chen gratefully lifting up the tea to moisten his parched throat. He knew enough from his training with Miss Haddie, that a lesson was about to be taught, so he waited to hear what wisdom Chen had to share with him.

While also sipping the tea, Chen, without even looking up, spoke.

"You know they can smell fear or worry, don't you?"

"Are you talking about those wolves?" Galen asked.

"Yes, they can smell it when we yield to fear. It attracts them," Chen explained.

Taking a moment to consider what Chen just said, Galen sipped from his mug once more before he responded. He realized what Chen was referring to.

"I was worried about my parents and concerned about finding food and firewood for my friends. Right?"

"Yes. I'm sure you can figure out a better way than carrying all those concerns for the safety and care of others," Chen encouraged him. Silently, Galen searched his heart for the right answer to his worries.

"I guess I wasn't trusting Elemet in his ability to care for my parents and my friends. I was taking on that burden and allowing fear to disturb my peace. Is that it?"

"Very good," Chen applauded him. "You must remember that if you have been sent elsewhere, Elemet will most definitely care for those you must leave behind. Remember my reassurances to Shoshanna regarding her own father's well-being? Nothing is missed and nothing is overlooked, even in your own provision. Sometimes your provision might appear in different ways and through other methods, but it will be there, nonetheless. Can you see this now?"

"Yes. So how am I to respond when I feel that discomfort or warning in my soul?"

"Take it to Elemet and ask him to care for these needs rather than allowing nervousness or fear to settle into your soul. As I said earlier, fear or worry attracts darkness and darkness is more than willing to respond. In this smoking mountain region, it is especially important to pay attention to whether you are led by light with total confidence in Elemet's ability to take care of all things, or darkness will work its way in to respond to your fears or worry."

As Chen spoke, once again, Galen found himself drawn into the depths of his eyes. Rather than glancing away as before, Galen allowed the swirling light to completely saturate every part of his being. The lie of self-confidence was brought to the surface and quickly washed away in his love. Feeling almost dizzy from the intensity cleansing his soul, he shut his eyes briefly to regain his balance. When he opened them again, Chen was gone.

Quickly, Galen arose to arouse his friends so they could enjoy the morning feast Chen had provided for them and to tell them about the things he had already learned that morning.

By mid-morning, all four of the friends sat around the toasty fire sipping their warm mugs of tea after enjoying a hearty breakfast, nearly fit for a king. Galen shared his experiences that morning and afterward, the other three commented on the importance of this new revelation.

"So what you are saying," Roany responded, "is that darkness, and that pack of wolves, can smell fear or worry at all times, right?" Galen nodded his head as he took another sip from his mug. "That almost makes me afraid to be afraid."

Galen almost choked on his tea as he tried to keep from laughing. "Roany, I don't think that is the point. I think we just need to focus on how loved we are, cast any concerns to Elemet, and then trust him to take care of everything else. At least that's what Chen told me."

"That is really important to remember as we progress onward," Shoshanna commented. "I certainly don't want to find myself surrounded by wolves. Maybe if we focused on being thankful, we wouldn't be tempted to worry."

Uri had been listening to the discussion for some time before he finally added his thoughts on the matter. "I know what I'm going to do," he added with a shrug of his shoulders. "It's simple. Don't think. Just walk and then we will be fine."

The other three had to laugh a little at Uri's conclusions.

"If that works for you," Galen smiled, "then I suggest you do it."

With all their needs fully met that morning, they decided to pack up whatever leftovers remained to carry with them for when they got hungry again later on down the trail. It was time for them to continue down the rocky path before them, though each wondered when this journey would arrive at their destination. At Chen's reference to the "region," they were currently in, they secretly hoped that the hardest part of their endeavors were behind them. Until told otherwise, though, they knew their attention had to be very clearly focused on trusting, being thankful, and following where they were led.

Chapter Nine

EYES TO SEE

Absolutely delighted to meet a friend of Yona's, Ms. Bina directed Yona to bring out her best serving dishes and fancy cups she had stashed away. A lace table cloth with embroidered flowers was laid across her table while the sweet cinnamon cookies with swirls were brought out and placed upon a serving plate for the event. Jessah helped by lighting the special candles and pouring the hot water for their tea. Finally, when all was prepared the three gathered the around table.

As they nibbled on cookies and drank their hot tea, Jessah, sensing that this might be the right time to share the most recent of her adventures, told the other two about her second flight on the golden eagle so she could visit with them.

"What? You got to fly on that huge eagle again?" Yona nearly dropped the cookie she was holding. "Is he close by? Can I see him?"

"He landed in a clearing not far from here, but I'm quite certain he took off again as soon as I left," Jessah explained. "He is probably flying high above the clouds waiting until I am finished here. Miss Haddie said the eagle would know when I was done and ready to leave."

Upon hearing the name of Miss Haddie mentioned, Ms. Bina spoke up.

"Oh child, you must tell me all about Haddie," she requested. "It has been such a long time since I have seen her."

Not quite sure on how much she could tell Ms. Bina, Jessah decided to reveal only very general information about her. "Miss Haddie is amazing. She wanted me to send you her greeting."

"I'm quite sure she is doing wonderfully," Ms. Bina remarked. "She has lived quite a remarkable life. You know, the two of us are actually sisters."

"What? How many years has it been since you last saw your sister?" Yona asked.

"Oh, it has been a great many years," Ms. Bina admitted. "The village elders selected a fine young man for me to marry, a doctor who made his rounds caring for those sick or injured. When I married, Haddie suddenly moved away. She was younger than me and would have been next on the list of potential wives. Haddie would have nothing to do with the whole system, so naturally, I never saw her except for very brief visits where she'd bring me some of her tea."

The two young girls looked at each other in shock. Miss Haddie had never mentioned she had a sister. Jessah wondered if it was just too hard for Miss Haddie to talk about. Ms. Bina continued.

"Just before my husband passed away several years back, I noticed a change in him. Something was bothering his conscience and it took him a long time to tell me what it was. All he told me was there were times when he was permitted to heal people and then there were times when they suddenly became ill and he was not allowed to help them. It was shortly after that confession, he himself became ill and died. Following his death, my eyesight began failing, so here I sit in the dark, even when it is light outside."

"I'm so sorry," Jessah said. "I lost both my parents in an accident in the forest, and I'm sure Yona has told you about her loss as well." Compelled by a burst of compassion for the woman, Jessah suddenly stood up and moved around the table next to Ms. Bina.

"You know, I have excellent eyesight and maybe Elemet might permit you to see some of what I see. Would you let me hold your hands?"

"Oh, my dear. That is so sweet, but my eyes and body are just too old. I expect that I will be sitting in the dark until I finally pass on as my husband has."

"I'm sorry, but I don't believe it has to be like that for you. I'm sure Miss Haddie told you about Elemet, and he is telling me right now that he is willing to let you see again. Will you hold my hands? That's not too hard, is it?"

Feeling in the air for Jessah's hands, Ms. Bina responded. "I guess if you feel so strongly about it, you can go ahead and hold my hands, dear."

Taking hold of the wrinkled hands, Jessah looked upward with her eyes closed. Her mouth was moving in silent conversation with Elemet for a moment when suddenly Ms. Bina gave a little shout.

"What is it, Ms. Bina?" Yona inquired jumping to her feet to stand beside the old woman. "Are you alright?"

"Oh, I'm fine, Yona," Ms. Bina assured her. "I just felt a jolt go through me for a moment. Nothing to worry about."

As the two girls stood beside Ms. Bina, suddenly the old woman spoke up. "Wait a moment. I think I am seeing something." Both Yona and Jessah watched in awe as the woman described the sights exactly as Jessah had seen while flying on the back of the eagle!

"I can see the blue skies above Kumani with white clouds rushing by. It is so beautiful!" she exclaimed. "Oh, I can see some of the villages below you! Wow! It looks like one of the cabins has been burnt down recently. So sad! Now, I'm seeing another cabin with someone working on the roof with an older couple standing outside watching. Yes, now I see the clearing where the eagle landed and you walking towards Chana. This is amazing, Jessah! It's like I can see through your eyes! So, tell me about all that I saw."

"Well," Jessah explained as they dropped their hands, "you saw the blue skies and clouds that I saw as I flew here."

"But what about the burnt ruins of that cabin? What happened there?" Ms. Bina inquired.

"That cabin once belonged to Oren, my friend's father, but the enforcers burned it to the ground when he would not help them pursue his daughter and friends."

"Wait!" Yona interrupted. "You say the enforcers burned down the cabin?"

"Yes. That is what Oren told us," Jessah replied.

"Well, the village elders and their messengers are spreading a whole different story!" Yona stated. "That reminds me! I have something I need to read to you that might be important. Let me get that paper and I will be right back." Yona exited the room to collect the information she had. While she was out of the room, Ms. Bina asked Jessah for one more favor.

"Could we hold hands one more time so I could see Haddie's face? I so miss her and almost wish that I had responded as she did to all the village elders' directives so we could be working together rather than separated these many years."

"That will be up to Elemet. I have no control over what you see and what you don't see, but we could try." The child reached over and grabbed Ms. Bina's hands and waited to see what would occur. As she watched the old woman, a smile moved across her face.

"I see her!" she exclaimed. "I see Haddie! Oh, she looks so wonderful and happy. I can also see the inside of her cottage. Oh, it is so lovely!" After a few moments of enjoying the sight, she dropped hands with the young girl just as Yona was returning with her paper in hand.

"I found it! I finally found where I had put it," Yona announced.

"So, what does all this have to do with Oren's house being burned down by the enforcers?" Jessah asked.

"Well, when I went to the marketplace in Chana for some supplies, there was a man making an announcement about their need for more enforcers," Yona explained.

"Yona," Ms. Bina interrupted. "I wonder if I might be able to see what you saw in the marketplace if you would hold my hands as Jessah did. I would like to know what is going on in my village as well. Would you mind?"

"Of course not!" Yona replied as she handed Jessah the paper and then stood in front of Ms. Bina. As soon as the two held hands, once again Ms. Bina was able to see all the activity in the marketplace that Yona had seen only days before.

She saw the young men looking over Yona, the announcement being made, and the poster with the names and sketches of the dissenters.

"So tell me, what was that man saying?" Ms. Bina inquired.

"He said some dissenters had escaped, THEY burned down the cabin, and now have a bounty on their heads," Yona explained. "I wrote down the names for you, Jessah, just in case you needed to know who they are looking for."

"Oh, thank you for that," Jessah replied. "Miss Haddie and Oren will be very interested in this information for sure."

Ms. Bina shook her head in disgust after Yona released her hands. "I can't believe how the people in my village can get so stirred up and are so easily swayed by every-thing the village elders say! This really disturbs me quite a bit, my dears." Both girls could see that the woman was considering something.

"Jessah, would you mind delivering a message to my sister when you see her again?"

"Of course!"

"Would you let her know that I now fully support all she is doing in following Elemet? I, too, would like to follow Elemet. With my eyesight as limited as it is, I don't know what I could do, but my home is open to anyone needing a place to stay. I know it is a little late for my decision, but I can't just sit here and do nothing as the village elders con-tinue to do whatever they think is right. Would you please tell her that, child?"

"I will, Ms. Bina. And the next time I visit, I would be happy to report to you everything she says."

"Oh, bless you, Jessah! Would you mind coming near so I can give you a hug before you leave? I so enjoyed getting to know you and look forward to visiting with you again!"

Jessah walked across the room and gave the woman a hug. As they embraced, she looked up into her friend's face and noticed tears welling up in joy. After saying their goodbyes, Yona walked Jessah to the back door so she could make her return flight with the eagle back to Miss Haddie's homestead. The two friends embraced one last time with Jessah promising it would not be too long before her next visit.

The afternoon sun was moving closer to the horizon as Jessah clung to the mighty eagle soaring through the skies. Even as the wind whistled past her ears, her mind was very preoccupied with all the information she had gathered both during her earlier flight and at Ms. Bina's home that morning. She was anxious to get back to learn from Miss Haddie what needed to be done next.

Chapter Ten

CONSIDERING THEIR CHOICES

Her cabin felt so dark and empty as Tanzi wandered from room to room looking for any new personal items belonging to Roany. As she rustled through his belongings, she was searching for a clue as to where he might be hiding out with his friends. Pangs of loneliness hit her every so often as she touched and looked over everything that reminded her of her only child. Did I really do the right thing, she wondered.

As soon as that thought popped in, an even stronger thought entered into her mind.

"You had no other choice, but to stir the village elders to action," it said reminding her of how many times the elders were willing to hold back and do little when they needed to act. Still convinced that Roany was not in his right mind, but rather was swayed by the influence of his misguided friends, she had to agree with this new thought. As she meditated on this, a swirling gray cloud formed around her until it completely encapsulated her encircling her entire body a number of times before it vanished from sight.

Completely unaware of what had just occurred, Tanzi felt a new resolve come upon her as she searched Roany's belongings with focus. Suddenly, she came upon an old parchment of her son's which detailed some of the dreams he had at various times and then mentioned some of the discussions he and Galen had throughout their many years of friendship. Her heart beat faster as she realized this might be the very thing to assist the enforcers in finding the missing group. Sitting down, Tanzi carefully studied the most recent of her son's entries.

Oren was a little nervous as he started out on his first adventure after spending time with Miss Haddie. As was typical, she had insisted he was ready to step out and try his newly acquired abilities. Though she had all confidence in his ability to succeed, he did not.

As he pushed his way through the branches and brush surrounding the trails, he recalled her instructions. Miss Haddie made it clear that he would only gain confidence by exercising his new gifts. Thus far on his journey, he had no need to step into the uncommon ways he was growing more familiar with. For that he was thankful.

He loved the forests and the outdoors all around him. After working for years in the stuffy, old butcher shop with the smell of raw meat and fish saturating even the clothing he wore, he was thrilled to enjoy the outdoors, despite the stagnant, smoky scent lingering in the air about him. The light directing him was refreshing, especially since he now understood it was worth trusting as he walked.

It didn't take too long for him to arrive at his destination, which required careful observation before he could approach his target. Standing back in the cover of the forest, Oren watched as Mendi, cleaned up the unused debris from the roof repairs he made to Eber and Giza's home earlier that day. As Oren studied the young man from a distance, he sensed a warning to use extreme caution not to be detected by him. Double-checking his position making certain that only his eyes were exposed, he continued observing the interaction between the older couple and this well-built man easily moving logs and lumber around the property as if it were nothing.

Gaging the couple to be in their late fifties or early sixties, Oren could see how this strong young laborer could appear to be a godsend helping them with their more physical tasks around the house. His smile and demeanor seemed to put the pair quite at ease. He watched as Giza brought out some freshly baked cookies for both the young man and her husband to enjoy as the property around the home was put in order.

Eventually, the young man finally took his leave and headed out from their property obviously heading to his own home in town. However, from his vantage point, Oren could see that the young man, as soon as he was out of sight from the cabin, met with several other individuals on the path heading out of the meadow. After conferring together, the first young man continued on his way while the other two split up encircling the perimeter of the meadow as if they were looking for someone.

Realizing that he would soon be in danger of discovery by one of the searchers, he decided it might be time to put one of his newest gifts into practice. Moving close to a large tree, Oren closed his eyes and looked around for the doorway he needed. There it was! Taking one step inside the door way, he found himself in a beautiful location where lights swirled and clouds danced around him just as it did when he was with Miss Haddie.

Though he was standing in another dimension, he could still hear the twigs breaking and the dry leaves crunching under the feet of the man passing by his hidden location. Oren waited until the silence returned before stepping forward returning him to his original hiding spot among the trees.

Crouching down, he watched as the two men met at the conclusion of their search and then headed off on the path heading towards town. He realized that Galen's parents, Eber and Giza, were being used as bait just in case any of the dissenters decided to come and check on them. Their "handyman" was nothing more than someone trying to get in good with them so he could assist in capturing Galen, his daughter, and their friends.

Rage surfaced within him as he considered the whole evil plot the village elders had cooked up to capture their "prey." At first, as his emotions rose up inside, the peace he treasured began waning. Suddenly, he was brought back to attention by the resounding words of Miss Haddie in his head.

"We can't be moved by what we see or feel in this adventure, or we will be led astray by our natural senses," he recalled her saying. "We are only led by what we hear Elemet saying and follow his lead at all times."

Taking a deep breath, Oren made a conscious effort to focus once again on his directive. He was simply to observe what was happening at the cabin and then see if he might be able to safely make contact with Eber and Giza.

Watching the cabin and the region around them for any further signs of activity, he felt a clear urging to continue with his original plan. All was safe. Oren, with sweat beading up on his brow, moved quickly through the meadow and knocked on the front door.

Giza responded to his knocking and opened the door, a little surprised to have another visitor so soon after their handyman had just left.

"Hello ma'am," the gray-haired man greeted her. "I'm a little new at this, so please excuse my awkwardness. I believe you have met my daughter, Shoshanna, a little while back. I need to let you know what has since happened to our family and what could be happening to your family next. May I come in, please?"

Opening the door, Giza and Eber permitted their new guest to enter. For the next hour, Oren described the plot and trap that was being set around them to capture their son.

Chapter Eleven

REPORTING THE NEWS

The back door burst open just as Miss Haddie was preparing some tea. Excitedly, Jessah entered the cottage breathless and eager to report all that had occurred on her recent mission.

"Come in and sit for a moment, child," Miss Haddie encouraged her. "You look a bit wind-blown and troubled."

Jessah bit her lip realizing she was stirred up and needed to collect her thoughts for a moment so she could accurately detail the events of the day. She waited as Miss Haddie poured each of them a cup of tea and sat down across from her. Taking a breath, and then sip from the warm brew, Jessah could feel the peace pour down upon her as she rested for a moment. Once the woman could sense calmness upon the young girl, she urged her to start at the beginning describing all that she had seen while flying on the back of the eagle.

"I saw what was left of Oren and Shoshanna's cabin," she began. "Only ashes and some debris were left behind, just as Oren suspected." Miss Haddie nodded as Jessah continued. "From there, I recognized Galen's cabin where I saw some young man working on their roof for them. I don't really know why, but that made me feel uncomfortable."

"Yes, there has been a plan put in place to try and capture Galen and the others should they attempt to visit his parents again," Miss Haddie explained, "but not to worry. Oren has already been sent to warn Eber and Giza if they will only listen. We shall see how things went when he returns. Now, what about your visit with Yona? How did that go?"

"Oh, that went very well," Jessah responded. "I learned some very interesting things there. First, Yona informed me that the village elders sent out a messenger to Chana and she overheard him say that a bounty had been placed on the heads of the escaped dissenters. He also said that they were looking for new enforcers to help capture them. In fact, the man called them "dangerous" and said the dissenters had burned down Oren's cabin."

"Yes, that sounds like the way darkness works. They twist the truth just a little for their own benefit to help agitate the emotions of the people to their favor," Miss Haddie commented.

"But that is not all!" Jessah added. "They also put up a poster with names and sketches of the dissenters they are looking for. Yona wrote down the names on the poster for us," she said while handing Miss Haddie the parchment Yona had given her.

"Hmm. Very interesting!" she stated while looking over the names. "Well, we certainly can see who the instigator behind all this is." Reading the list out loud, she continued. "Galen, Shoshanna, Uri, and now Oren has been added to the list with no mention of Roany."

Sadly shaking her head, Miss Haddie commented, "Poor Tanzi. I can only imagine the pain and anger she must be feeling at the loss of her son and her planned future for him. Guilt will soon be following when she recognizes the pointlessness of all her efforts. Roany has chosen for himself and she cannot reverse that. We shall see which way she chooses as things progress."

"There was something else I learned during my visit with Yona and Ms. Bina," Jessah inserted in their discussion. "You never told me that Ms. Bina was your sister!"

"Yes, I did grow up in a family before coming out here, but that was very long ago."

"So now that we have met, I would love to hear the whole story from your side," Jessah pleaded.

"It's not really too complex to explain. Bina was content to follow the desires of the village elders, and I was not. Much like Shoshanna, I left in search of the truth. In the midst of my searching, Elemet found me. I have come to love him and his ways so much better."

"And what about Ms. Bina's husband? She mentioned that while working as a doctor, something started to bother him, though he never told her what that was. She said after that, he grew weak and died. What was that about?"

"Yes, Yanis was a decent man who enjoyed helping people get better," Miss Haddie explained. "Unfortunately, there were some unethical things that the village elders asked Yanis to do as a doctor. At first, he complied, but after a while, his conscience could no longer push his convictions aside. When he refused to act, the village elders took action and he shortly died."

"What does that mean?" Jessah pressed her. "What did they ask him to do?"

"Well child, even Ms. Bina is unaware of the terrible position he was put in as a doctor under the dictates of the village elders. Let's just say, that not everyone who died on this island died of natural causes."

"Is that what happened to Shoshanna's mother as well?" Jessah asked in horror.

"Jessah, there are a great many terrible things that darkness wants to do in the lives of people. Not all are willing participants, but fear has held them captive to do as it directs. Rather than focusing on the pain and loss caused by this blindness to the truth, we need to instead look at what we can do to bring truth to others so this cycle can end in their lives as well."

"Both Yanis and Dara, Shoshanna's mother, may not be here on the island of Kumani, but they are not completely gone. The same is true for your parents. Their response or desire for truth while here on this island dictates another kind of future for them. We never have to be afraid of leaving this island at any point. Elemet is watching and he has a secure future for us whether we continue here fulfilling our destiny or are moved to another place where each person is valued and treasured with him for all eternity."

Tears formed in Jessah's eyes as her heart filled with a fresh outpouring of love and peace regarding her own parents and the loved ones of others no longer present.

"He is so wonderful!" For a few moments, Jessah was without words, and then she remembered what had happened with Ms. Bina during her visit.

"Oh, I must tell you! When Ms. Bina was talking about how she now sits in complete darkness because of her eyes, I felt compelled to hold her hands while I spoke with Elemet. As we held hands, she suddenly was able to see what I had seen during my flight with the eagle!" Jessah explained with wide eyes. "Then when Yona held her hands, she was able to see what was going on in their village!"

"That is beautiful, Jessah. I must admit in all my years that is the first time I have heard of that occurring. I am so happy Bina was able to see through the eyes of others."

"But that is not all," the girl continued. "Ms. Bina also said she would now like to follow Elemet just like you and is opening her home for anyone needing a place to stay during their journeys in the region."

Now it was Miss Haddie's turn to tear up as she heard of her own sister's desire for Elemet.

"The only problem is, how will she be able to journey here so you can teach her the ways of the eagle just like you did with me? She is quite old and her eyes only work when we are holding her hands."

"That is quite true, my dear. I believe that I must go to her so she may learn."

Astonished at that idea, Jessah asked, "Are you going to walk all the way there, or fly on the back of the eagle like me?"

"Actually, I believe Elemet has another way for me to go to her," Miss Haddie smiled. "This way will be much quicker and more efficient for the two of us aging ladies. I must wait for his timing on this."

Jessah knew better than pressing Miss Haddie any further. She would certainly discuss this new plan with her when it was time.

Chapter Twelve

LOOKING GOOD

I t had now been several days since Galen's encounter with the wolves, Chen's intervention, and the much-needed instruction that followed. The journey through the smoking mountains continued to add mental exhaustion to the foursome even as the physical exertion of their upward climb took its toll upon their bodies. The food they had been given days back had diminished rapidly until, once again, they found their supply low forcing their provision to be divided up into portions.

Tensions ran high as each of them battled to keep from snapping at each other over minor things that came up. Growling stomachs only added to their discomfort. Finally, as they pressed on, Uri spotted something that made him stop in his tracks. Just down the hill from where they were on the mountain trail grew another apple tree heavy with fruit.

Once Uri stopped, the others also came to a halt as they all gazed at the luscious-looking fruit. As Galen and Roany studied the rough terrain looking for an easy way down and back, they came to the conclusion that climbing down to the tree would just be too dangerous for them to attempt. Shoshanna was too tired to care much, but Uri could not get his eyes off the prize.

"I could make it down there easy," Uri boasted. "Just tie one of the ropes around me and hold on as I work my way down."

"Uri, I don't think we should attempt this," Galen responded. "Look how steep it is and all the loose gravel everywhere. Your feet would slip out from under you for sure."

"Think about it! Here we are starving as we go with very little food left and then we see this tree loaded with fruit. Don't you think this might be Elemet's way of providing for us?" Uri countered.

"I don't know. With us being as tired and weak as we feel right now, I'm not sure we could pull this off. What do you think, Roany?" Galen asked.

"The apples do look mighty good," Roany admitted. Finally, Shoshanna had caught her breath enough to add her opinion into the discussion.

"I don't think we should do this," she cautioned. "I don't see anything indicating this is the way we are supposed to go. And who knows? Maybe the answer we need is right around the next corner."

"But we are right here!" Uri exclaimed. "We can see the apples from where we stand! Roany, you and I can do it. Get your rope out and you can tie it around me. I will be down and back up before you know it!"

Too tired to discuss it any further, Roany pulled out the rope he carried and carefully tied it around Uri's waist. As Uri started working his way downward, Roany looked towards Galen hoping he would assist in holding the rope with him. With a grunt in frustration, Galen dropped his knapsack beside Shoshanna and walked over to Roany's side to help. The two friends wrapped the rope around a large stone to help hold Uri's weight as he negotiated his way down the slippery hillside.

Crumbling stone tumbled down the mountainside nearly creating a landslide beneath him, but Uri pressed on grabbing ahold of anything that appeared stable enough to help keep him upright. Just as it appeared he was about to make contact with the fruit-laden tree, the rope snapped on a sharp edge of a stone sending Uri tumbling a short distance down the side of the mountain.

"Uri!" Shoshanna screamed as his body crushed against a lone, mid-sized tree with roots barely holding into the loose soil around it. The three stood terrified as they recognized how precarious his position was. If the roots gave way, Uri would certainly fall to his death on the jagged rocks below him.

"Uri, are you okay?" Galen called down.

It was several seconds before he could respond. "I think I may have cracked some ribs. Hurts bad. It's hard to breathe."

"We've got to get him back up here," Galen stated. "I think we have another rope in my knapsack. If we tie the two pieces together and make a loop for Uri to put over himself, maybe we could all pull him back up."

The three quickly worked tying the ropes together so it could reach Uri.

"How are you doing, Uri?" Galen called out. "We're almost ready to drop a rope down to you." With the rope securely wrapped around another stone, the end was slowly lowered down until Uri was able to grab it. Placing one arm into the loop and over his head, Uri, though in great pain, climbed up as they all pulled their friend back to the trail.

Once he was secured and sitting on one of the boulders, Galen checked his injuries. When his shirt was lifted, the skin was already discolored. Uri groaned in agony. While Shoshanna sat with him offering sips of water, Roany and Galen stepped aside to discuss their dilemma.

"Uri is in no condition to continue walking right now," Roany confided to Galen.

"I know, I know. We may have to set up camp somewhere nearby until we get some instruction on how to proceed. Would you mind scouting around to see if there is a good spot to camp out close by?

"Sure. I'll be back soon to report what I've found." With that, Roany strolled off up the trail ahead to see if there was a convenient place for them to spend the night. Once Roany left, Galen returned to Uri's side. Shoshanna had wetted a small cloth napkin and was patting Uri's brow as he groaned with every breath.

"Roany is checking the trail ahead to see if there is a good spot for us to camp for the night," Galen explained to them.

"Oh good, because I'm pretty sure I won't be able to do much walking right now."

"I understand. We wouldn't expect you to after a fall like that," Galen assured him.

As Shoshanna sat beside the two men, she suddenly noticed the palms of her hands were turning bright red feeling as though they were on fire.

"What is going on?" she asked, looking at Galen. Galen pulled her hands closer towards him for a closer inspection.

"I'm not sure. Something is happening. Give me a moment." Galen shut his eyes to get some better clarity. After listening for a moment, he had a suggestion.

"I think you are supposed to put your hands on Uri's injured side," Galen responded.

"Wait! No one is putting their burning hands on me right now! I'm in enough pain as it is!" Uri exploded.

"Uri, listen. I think Elemet wants to help you," Galen calmly responded. "There is nothing else we can do to help relieve your pain right now, so I suggest you let Shoshanna put her hands on you and see what happens. It might help. With all you have already suffered, how much worse could a little heat be?"

With the intensity of the pain only increasing, Uri nodded his head in agreement. Gingerly, Galen lifted up Uri's shirt once again. Shoshanna gasped noticing the growing discoloration on his side. She knew this was serious.

Taking a breath, she laid her burning hands upon his side. Uri screamed in pain as the heat penetrated his body. As she continued holding her hands in place, she felt the intensity of the heat increase for a time. At this point, Uri only groaned as it saturated his entire side.

Shoshanna closed her eyes and was amazed as she seemed to peer inside Uri's body. She saw broken bones mending and the tissue around the injury returning to normal. When she opened her eyes and removed her hands, the discoloration was quickly fading as she and Galen watched.

Uri also had his eyes closed. The pain slowly decreased. When he opened his eyes, both Galen and Shoshanna were staring at him.

"How do you feel?" Galen asked.

"Relaxed. Very, very relaxed," he replied, looking very sleepy.

"Any more pain?" Galen inquired.

"No. Nothing. I do feel a little weak, though. Could I just lay down for a moment?"

Quickly, Shoshanna grabbed a blanket from her knapsack and made a soft spot for Uri's head. He quietly rested as the two stepped aside to discuss what had just happened.

"Did you see that?" Shoshanna asked in shock. "What was that?"

Grabbing both of her hands, Galen turned them over to look at her palms one more time before speaking. "That was amazing! I think Uri is going to be absolutely fine once he gets up."

"That was Elemet, wasn't it?" Shoshanna clarified.

"Yes, that most definitely was. He is good. Wow!" That was all Galen could say. The two of them returned to Uri, sitting close by as he rested. They were in awe of what had just occurred.

By the time Roany returned, Uri was sitting upright and even laughing with the other two. Roany could hardly believe his eyes! Reporting back on what he had found, he let them know that just over the next hill, he discovered a beautiful campsite prepared for them with plenty of food, a warm fire burning, and everything already set up for the night. With relief and joy washing over all of them, the friends headed towards the campsite to enjoy their meal and some needed relaxation.

Later that night, after everyone had eaten, they sat around the fire laughing and chatting with each other. Desiring a few quiet moments, Shoshanna walked a short distance away from the men and sat down on a boulder.

The smoky haze had begun lifting and dissipating the higher they got in elevation so she was able to see the stars filling the night sky, something she had not been able to see her entire life. The stars mesmerized her as she identified clusters painting images in the heavens. The full moon peaked over the horizon showing its face which seemed to be smiling back at her.

While considering the events of the day, Shoshanna set down her cup and took a moment to again glance at the palms of her hands. They appeared as they always had, she thought to herself while turning them over. The heat they temporarily emitted stunned her, but even more shocking was the fact that Elemet had used her to accomplish his purposes. With thankfulness in her heart, she looked upward again searching the stars to see if maybe she might see traces of Elemet's face peering through them.

All was quiet and peaceful within and at that very moment, she suddenly sensed someone sitting next to her. Fully expecting it to be one of their group, she turned and was shocked to see Chen sitting next to her also staring at the night sky while sipping his own cup of tea.

"Chen! Where did you come from?" she asked surprised at his sudden appearance.

"Oh, I'm always around," he assured her. "You just don't always see me." After taking another sip of his cup, he commented, "That is quite a gift you have there."

"What?"

"The gift you used to bring healing to Uri."

"Oh! Yes, that really surprised me. I was not expecting that at all. I thought maybe Galen could do something like that," Shoshanna admitted, "but not me."

"Yes, Galen is very gifted as well, but Elemet chose you to have this gift," Chen responded.

"He did, but I don't understand why. I'm nobody special. I just needed to escape with the others so the enforcers would not capture us," she said.

"That is where you are very wrong, Shoshanna. You just don't fully know who you are yet," he stated while gazing into her eyes.

As she peered into his eyes, her fears of unworthiness were swallowed up by a fiery love that pulsated through her body. Prisms of light seemed to wrap around her causing everything else to fade. In this cocoon of love, she suddenly saw Elemet's face shining like the sun before her.

"You are my beloved daughter," he said. "There is much you will discover about yourself as you draw closer to the Eagles' Nest and your designed destiny."

Suddenly, the whole scene faded and she was back on the boulder alone staring at the night sky.

It took her a few moments to gain her composure enough to walk back over to her three companions still talking around the fire.

"I can see how I allowed my hunger and desire for what appeared good to lead me in making a bad decision," Uri admitted. "I need to remember to ask and listen to Elemet's directions all the time." Taking a breath, he continued. "I've got to remember that!"

"That's good," Galen encouraged him. "And didn't Shoshanna say the answer we needed could be just around the corner, and it was!" Suddenly Galen looked up and was taken back a little by the glow emanating around her. "Wow! What happened to you, Shoshanna? You look different!"

With a hint of a smile, Shoshanna quietly sat down near the fire as she steadied herself, still quite shaken by her encounter. The three men stared in silence waiting for her to speak.

"I saw Chen while I was sitting alone for a moment."

Immediately, the other three glanced around looking to see if Chen was still there.

"He's gone now," she assured them, "but he did say he is always around."

"Well, are you going to tell us what happened to you?" Roany asked. Nodding, Shoshanna continued.

"I was just enjoying the beauty of the stars and the night sky when I thought again about my hands becoming hot and then seeing Uri healed when I touched him. As I was wondering about all that, Chen was suddenly sitting beside me."

"He seems to do that a lot!" Uri added. Smiling at his comment, Shoshanna proceeded.

"I asked him why I had been given that gift and not one of you. He told me I just didn't know who I was yet. As I continued staring in his eyes, something left me, and then all this love came over me." Her voice choked up a little as she fought back the tears.

"That is amazing!" Galen responded, fighting some tears himself.

"I saw the face of Elemet," she continued with tears now flowing down her cheeks. "He called me his beloved daughter and said I would discover my designed destiny on this journey."

The three young men gazed at her changed appearance unable to comment further on her encounter. However, each of them secretly hoped that they might have a similar encounter as they progressed through the mountains towards their final destination.

Soberly, they decided it was time to retire for the night. Turning towards their own bedding, they laid down and closed their eyes to rest while dreaming of things beyond what they knew and a love that conquers all fear.

Chapter Thirteen

A MIDNIGHT VISITOR

Tossing and turning in her bed, Ms. Bina always had the hardest time at night, especially since the loss of her sight. Without the light indicating a new day had begun, everything seemed to blur together. Having Yona around did help her keep track of day and night to some degree. Her cheerful humming and friendly chatter throughout the day kept her mind quite busy, but at night, the deafening silence was hard to endure. She wondered how much longer before Yona would be up and preparing to make breakfast. It can't be too much longer, she consoled herself.

As she rolled over looking for a more comfortable position, she thought she heard shuffling across her bedroom floor.

"Yona? Is that you?" she asked, but got no response, so she asked again. "Child, is it already morning?"

"No sister, it is still in the middle of the night," came the reply.

With her heart racing in fear, Ms. Bina asked, "Who is this and what are you doing in my bedroom?"

"Don't be afraid, Bina. It's me, Haddie."

"Haddie! How did you get here? I know you live very far from Chana."

"I have been sent here by Elemet to answer some of your questions."

"Oh, my stars! Is it possible that you walked all that way to see me?" Pulling up a chair and patting her sister's hand, Haddie responded.

"I didn't actually walk here. I was brought here by Elemet."

"What does that mean?" Bina asked. "I'm not dreaming, am I?"

"You can feel my hand, can't you?" Bina conceded that she could feel her sister's hand and was finally convinced that she was indeed very real.

"Well, don't just sit there! Help me up so I can hug you! It has been way, way too long."

With Haddie's assistance, Bina was able to turn sideways and sit upright on her bed. The two sisters then were able to hug. Tears freely flowed as the two embraced for some time before another word was spoken. Finally, they released each other as Haddie handed a handkerchief to her sister to wipe the tears running down her cheeks.

After a short time of reminiscing, Haddie explained the purpose for which she had been sent.

"Jessah has informed me that you desire to know Elemet and even want to open your home to help those who are traveling through. Is this true?"

"Yes! Very true. While holding Jessah and Yona's hands, I was able to see a little of what is going on around me. I now realize how we had been manipulated for so long. You warned me about this all those years ago, but I was afraid and just decided to follow the directives of the village elders." Dropping her head a bit, Bina continued. "I was so blind back then and didn't want to see the truth right in front of me. Now I am blind and would love nothing more than to see the truth with my own eyes. Can you help me?"

Haddie smiled as she listened to her sister's heartfelt confession. Tears formed in her own eyes as she replied.

"Bina, it is never too late to come to the truth."

As the sisters sat together in the darkened room, Haddie briefly explained the history of the deception and then had the great honor of introducing Bina to the one who had always loved her. Once that was taken care of, Haddie revealed to Bina the new plan that emerged using her blindness as a cover of protection for herself and others.

Bina was delighted to be included!

"Elemet also says that in time, your sight will be fully restored, but until then, I will come regularly to continue training you in the ways of the eagle. You and Yona can also learn from Jessah as she comes by on occasion to visit. There will be others, but you will soon know as I do when someone is coming by."

The two sat and continued discussing all the things that were changing in Bina's life as new uncommon ways emerged. It was nearly dawn when Haddie finally informed her sister it was time for her to return back to her own homestead. After hugging once more time, Bina had another question.

"Do you think the time will come when I will be able to visit you in the same manner you were able to visit me?" she asked in hopeful expectation. "I would love to see where you have been living all these many years."

"Of course, sister! I am certain that Elemet will arrange for that to happen at some point, but for now, he has placed you in a very strategic position where you and Yona will be able to keep us informed of how things are developing here. There are many new gifts you will discover in the days ahead keeping you preoccupied until we meet again."

Suddenly remembering something she had, Haddie reached into her pocket and pulled out a brooch placing it into her sister's hand.

"What is it?" Bina asked.

"Let's see if you can feel what it is." Haddie watched as her sister methodically ran her fingers moving the item, feeling every swell and decline of its engraved shape.

"It's a brooch with some kind of bird engraved into it."

"Yes!" Haddie encouraged her. "It is an eagle with out-spread wings soaring in the air. This can serve as a reminder of our visit this evening and all we have discussed. You have now begun your training in the ways of the eagle, my sister!"

Bina was overjoyed with her gift and carefully wrapping her fingers around her new treasure as Haddie gently assisted her sister to lie back down in her bed. With great compassion, she tucked the blankets around Bina before leaving the room.

Yona was just waking right at that same moment. With her eyes still a little blurred from sleep, she glanced out her open bedroom door. Blinking, she thought she saw a woman walking out of Ms. Bina's room, however, as she watched, the woman suddenly disappeared!

Immediately, the young girl was up, rushing over to Ms. Bina's room making certain she was fine. As she stepped into the room, she sensed a sweet lingering presence that took her breath away. Glancing at Ms. Bina, Yona noticed that the older woman was sleeping peacefully with a huge smile on her face. As she studied her wrinkled face, Yona could almost detect a slight glow about it. Seeing Ms. Bina was obviously fine, she dismissed the shadowy figure of the woman supposing it only the tail end of a dream.

It was much later that morning when Ms. Bina finally started to stir. Yona was relieved to see that she had awakened and rushed to assist her in getting up. As she gently guided the woman to a chair, Ms. Bina casually mentioned that she had a guest last night. Thinking it was only a part of her dream, Yona just smiled as the woman settled into her seat.

As Yona stepped back, Ms. Bina held out her treasure before her.

"What is that?" she asked.

"Look at it," Ms. Bina encouraged her.

Yona carefully lifted the brooch out of her hand to study it. Her eyes grew big as she recognized this was not something she had previously owned.

"Where did you get this?"

"My visitor gave it to me so I could remember all that we discussed last night."

"And who was your visitor?" Yona asked.

"Haddie, my sister."

Yona's mouth dropped open as she realized that she had actually seen her visitor earlier that morning, though only briefly. "That is amazing! You must tell me everything she told you! I so want to know more about the way of the eagle as well!"

The two had much to talk about that morning as Ms. Bina recounted all that had occurred.

Chapter Fourteen

CONDEMNING EVIDENCE

The mood was tense as hooded figures filed into the large building hidden deep in the forests. No one wanted to show their faces if at all possible. The identity of village elders throughout the island of Kumani had always been a carefully guarded secret so none of the residents could actually identify which of their neighbors made the important decisions for everyone else within the perimeter of their control.

Up until now, fear had been the most effective weapon in keeping individuals in check. However, even as they gathered for this secret meeting with village elders from all over the island, one could sense the mounting frustration. How was it possible that a handful of rebels could continue to escape their clutches?

Rumors were flying and people everywhere were talking about the two escaped prisoners that no one could find. Stories were shared of a butcher and a blacksmith-in-training walking away from their assigned jobs with no sign of where they went. And now villagers were also discussing the young woman who simply did not show up for her presentation before the elders.

If left unchecked, people all over the island just might think that they also could break out of prison, walk away from their assignments, and young women might get the idea that they did not have to accept the decisions of elders for their lives. This was simply unheard of! Something had to be done quickly before these "successful dissenters" became heroes in the eyes of the people!

Tanzi had been summoned to give a reasonable explanation as to why none of the people they were searching for had been caught, though newly-recruited enforcers had been combing the habitable regions of the island. As the fire burned behind her, fire also burned within the eyes of the elders seated before their informant. They awaited her answer to the things now threatening the very fiber of their way of life for generations.

One hooded figure stood calling the meeting to order. The angry mutters of the hoods finally diminished as the presiding elder reminded them all of the purposes for their gathering that night.

"Gentlemen, you have been called here tonight to discuss a growing problem here on the island of Kumani," he began. "You all are aware of some difficulties we have been facing in some of our villages. We are concerned that fear and enforced submission is losing its grip upon the people we have dominated for so long. The secrecy of our domination has granted us many privileges and rights that none of us are ready to relinquish at this time. Isn't this true?"

Angrily the men responded affirmatively. One man in the back stood to his feet asking the question each of them had been discussing among themselves from the moment they first came together.

"So what are you going to do about this?" he called out. "We need to find these missing people and make an example of them before things really get out of hand!" As he sat down, another man rose to his feet as well.

"How is it with all the additional enforcers we have rounded up, we have not been able to capture any of these dissenters? I mean, this is an island! Where could they possibly go preventing us from capturing them all?"

"Yes, yes, yes!" the presiding elder responded. "I understand your frustration. And believe me, we all felt the same way. That is why we have summoned Tanzi, the one who first reported all this to us, to give us an explanation as to why none of our efforts have succeeded thus far. I believe she has brought us some new information which may assist us in capturing these rebels."

Taking one step back, the chief elder motioned for Tanzi to stand before the men with her new discoveries. Boldly, Tanzi stepped forward and once again drew back her hood allowing her glistening black hair to reflect the light from the fire behind her.

"Good evening, gentlemen," she began, hoping that what she had learned would suffice their growing concerns.

"In continuing my research as to where these missing dissenters may be, I have gathered some information that may be helpful to all of us."

"First, I wanted to say that posters have been put up in each of your villages with names and drawings of the missing dissenters, including the young woman, Shoshanna and her father, Oren. Oren is the missing butcher and Shoshanna is the young woman who missed her presentation before the elders that islanders have been talking about. Also on the posters are Galen and Uri, both escaped dissenters from one of our prisons."

"And what about the missing blacksmith?" one of the men called out from the crowd. "Isn't that your son, Roany? Why isn't his name and drawing on those posters as well? Are you trying to cover up for him?"

"No! Let me explain!" she said, a little surprised at the accusations. "Roany was duped by his friend, Galen. He's not a dissenter, just a little unwise right now."

"But aren't all dissenters duped by someone?" the man continued, roaring in irritation. "How is your son any different from the others, and how do we know you aren't trying to deceive us right now?"

"Sir, let me assure you, I have information that may turn the tables on our search for the dissenters if you will just let me proceed," she retorted. Taking a breath to regain her focus, Tanzi continued.

"First, we have already established an infiltrator with Galen's parents in the village of Kieran. He has befriended the couple and plans to stay close just in case Galen or any of the others decide to make contact with them. Other enforcers are sweeping the area around their house in case any of them show up."

Most of the elders seemed to approve as they nodded their heads, though some still maintained their doubts regarding her credibility. Tanzi continued.

"I have also been checking with those directing the enforcers on their search. They have informed me that they came across the very group we are looking for on the edge of the smoking mountains. They did mention that the smoke was very dense there and somehow the group slipped past them, so we are looking for individuals who are willing to venture into that region to continue the search there."

"Ha! There won't be many wanting to head into that region, for sure!" one man sarcastically responded.

"And that is why we have put a bounty on each of their heads," Tanzi countered. Again the men muttered under their breath to each other, wondering if even that would work. Tanzi continued.

"Now, the most important part of my discovery. Knowing that this Galen and my son have been friends for some time, I decided to go through some of his writings just in case he wrote down some things that might be helpful to us."

"As I looked through his papers and parchments, I discovered two new details that might be useful. First, he mentioned a place called the Eagles' Nest that Galen had told him about. Unfortunately, there was no mention as to where that place may be, but obviously, it must be somewhere on this island."

"Well, if we don't know where it is, how are we going to find it?" another man shouted out mockingly. Several other men laughed at his comment.

Feeling a little perturbed with the elders, Tanzi decided to ignore his response and finish with the most valuable piece of information she had. "I also came across the name of a woman who may actually be behind the scenes directing all this rebellion. My son referred to her as "Miss Haddie."

"As I searched the records of all our citizens, I came across the name "Haddie," apparently a young woman who disappeared from among us some years ago. She must be quite elderly now. But in addition to the name "Haddie," I learned that Haddie has an older sister, living in the village of Chana. Her name is Bina. The woman is a widow now, but she was once married to Yanis, one of your "doctors," I believe. I have also learned that she is blind and has one of our older orphans taking care of her."

"Can you get to the point, Tanzi?" the chief elder chastened her. "We don't need a history lesson, just information on how we can catch the dissenters."

"I am getting to the point!" she responded, now clearly irritated with the elders and their impatience. "If Bina and Haddie are still in contact, we might be able to find Haddie and learn from her where these missing dissenters are."

"And how do you know this Haddie is behind this whole conspiracy?" one man demanded.

"What information would an old lady and her blind sister possibly have that could be helpful to us? It just seems to me that you are looking for other people to point fingers at just so we would overlook your own son's involvement!" a second man called out.

"No! I'm trying to help you!" she cried out in defense.

"Okay, okay, gentlemen. Let's not attack our informant," the chief elder cautioned them. "Some of her information might actually be helpful. To continue, we do have some other matters we need to discuss while we are all together."

Then turning to Tanzi, he said, "Thank you for your help. We will consider what you have said, so if you would excuse us, please?" Gesturing with his arm, he indicated it was time for Tanzi to leave.

Angry and insulted, Tanzi grabbed her lantern before storming out the door. She headed down a path in the darkened forest, not noticing the hooded figure that followed her out into the night. She muttered to herself calling the elders every derogatory name she could think of.

"They are such fools," she whispered. "They don't realize how important all that information was! Wait until I show them! I'll catch this "Haddie" myself and let them all see that I was right!"

Chapter Fifteen

PRESSING FORWARD

Trudging along the rocky terrain, the four travelers noticed as the elevation increased, so did their difficulty in catching their breaths. Much needed breaks were more frequent now as they periodically rested. With this increase of difficulty, the group couldn't help but notice the sheer cliffs that lay before them. As they looked ahead, they each secretly hoped they would not be required to climb those cliffs in order to finally arrive at their destination.

With nothing but apparent challenges before them, Uri had a difficult time staying motivated. He was about done for the day. With only limited portions of food allotted for them, hunger and exhaustion were setting in. As his motivation plummeted, Uri tried his best to convince everyone they needed to set up camp early so they could just rest.

"Uri, I thought for sure you were the tough one who would always push us on!" Roany rebuked him. "What is going on with you? Are you losing your nerve or what?"

Turning to look down upon his companion, his eyes flashing with irritation, Uri responded. "Are you calling me weak?"

"Maybe not physically weak, but there are other types of weakness, you know. I would call all this whining about a little walk rather pathetic, actually," Roany countered.

"Weakness is not even in my vocabulary," Uri boasted. "I'm as strong as and maybe even stronger than the rest of you! I just think we need to stop for the night."

"You have made your thoughts perfectly clear, Uri! Wow! I can see how you ended up in prison. Your mouth just never stops!"

"I may have ended up in prison, but at least my mother wasn't the one who stirred up this whole mess with the village elders and their enforcers!" Uri retorted.

Immediately shame, and then anger fell upon Roany as Uri's accusations rang true. Retaliation rose up in self-defense. "Well, at least I have a mother!"

His harsh words cut deep into Uri's soul causing even greater pain and anger to rise up pitting the two against one another.

Galen finally caught wind of the two men's exchange of words and turned back to confront both of them as they stood face to face, ready to let their fists start flying.

"Roany! Uri! Stop it!" he interjected. "We can't let thoughts and insults rile up our emotions right now. I know everyone is tired. And when we are this worn out, we have to be on guard even more. Remember what Chen told us about the dangers of giving over to fear and our unproductive thoughts? I'm pretty sure we can add exhaustion to that list as well. Come on, guys. Let's not do this."

Roany and Uri, both feeling a little ashamed of themselves, each took a step back from their face to face conflict. After a few moments of silence, Uri spoke first.

"I'm sorry I brought up your mother. I know you already feel bad about that."

"And I'm sorry I brought up about you not having a mother, and mentioned the fact that you were whining," Roany added with a little grin.

"Okay, okay," Galen intervened. "Whining or not, I know all of us are tired. Why don't we just stop for the night and set up camp?"

After bringing some resolution to the conflict, Galen suddenly noticed that Shoshanna was no longer with them. He glanced around, looking and didn't see her anywhere. Feeling a little panicked after calling her name and getting no response, Galen and the other two decided to split up and look for her in different directions. Uri took off to the left of the trail while Roany went to the right. Galen decided to check just over the crest in front of them.

As he reached the top of the hill, he looked down into a lovely mountain meadowland next to a creek. There Shoshanna sat peaceably by a crackling fire where a feast awaited the group. Once he spotted her, he called back to his friends encouraging them to follow him.

Rather than yelling down to her, Galen decided to talk to her in closer proximity. Once he got close enough to hold a conversation with her, he had a few questions.

"Shoshanna, we were looking for you. Why didn't you tell me where you were going?"

"The boys were engrossed with whining and arguing and then I noticed a gray mist coming over them. When I looked ahead, I saw the light directing us to move ahead, so I decided to follow it knowing you all would eventually follow it as well," she responded. "I also was reminded of what we have learned on this journey. If we will just press on beyond what we are comfortable with, we will discover what Elemet had planned for us all along," she explained. "Isn't this lovely?"

Looking around, Galen had to admit, this was indeed a beautiful oasis in the midst of a difficult climb.

"Yes, it certainly is." As he glanced back up at the top of the knoll, he saw the other two men and waved at them, urging them to come.

Before too long, all four sat around the fire with full stomachs after enjoying the feast prepared for them. Noticing the dying flames of the fire, Uri volunteered to gather some more fuel to keep the fire going throughout the night.

Dusk was already upon them as Uri walked alongside the cascading creek while scouring the region for brush or wood. As he moved along, he noticed the creek flowed from a mountain spring and headed towards it. Lush green grass carpeted the sides of the hill while lavender and yellow wildflowers dotted the landscape. As he approached, he saw the rippling surface of the pond reflecting the oranges and reds of the setting sun.

The darkened arms of the trees were silhouetted in stark contrast to the brilliant horizon around him. A few bramble bushes gripped the banks of the pond as the trickling spring bounced off the stones plunking into the water.

The scene was so peaceful, Uri had to remain as the relaxing sounds penetrated his weary body. As he stood, he suddenly realized he was not alone. Chen was standing beside him.

Feeling a little unnerved by his presence, Uri drew back.

"Uri, you don't have to be afraid of me," Chen reassured him. "Come. Let's sit here for a while."

Reluctantly, Uri followed Chen to several large stones next to the pond where they sat down. At first, nothing was said as they stared at the water running down the stones in different directions, but all ending up in the same pond.

"I know you had a difficult time growing up as you did," Chen began. "That wasn't easy maturing without parents to guide you along."

Uri tried to swallow the lump he was feeling in his throat as Chen touched on some of his most sensitive memories.

"I know that sometimes other children can be quite cruel as they lash out of their own pain," Chen continued. "That is why you work so hard to come across as tough and hard."

Uri dropped his head, nodding as Chen proceeded. "But I did not create you to carry around those large branches in order to defend yourself hoping to drive off fear. If you will trust me, you will soon discover that you will be defended by the light that causes all darkness to flee."

Tears welled up in Uri's eyes as Chen spoke the truth, uncovering some of his deepest secrets.

"Look at me," Chen encouraged him. Hesitantly, Uri looked up and gazed into the swirling blue eternity found in his eyes. Immediately, he was swallowed up in love as all his fears were disarmed. He saw himself laying down the many branches of self-defense he carried internally. Once that was accomplished, Chen spoke again.

"Uri, you no longer have to carry those branches as that is not who you are. Your name means 'my light' and that is who you are. You are a carrier of my light designed to dispel darkness and bring hope to those enslaved to lies they have believed as well. Is this what you want?"

Huge tears trickled down Uri's cheeks as he felt hidden fears melt away and the strength of love saturate his being. The rejected child of his past was released as he let go in order to embrace his future.

The fresh mountain air brought great refreshing to the three companions as the night sky closed in around them. Just as they were beginning to wonder about Uri, the man returned carrying an armload of logs to add to the fire.

"Wow!" Roany exclaimed. "Where did you find that?"

"It was a gift from Chen." Uri suddenly had the full attention of his three friends.

"Where did you see him?" Galen asked.

"He met me beside the mountain spring." Uri explained. "We talked for a while."

Shoshanna, taking a long hard look at Uri, was the first to notice something very different about him.

"Uri, you have a glow about you! Something has changed, hasn't it?"

Without words to accurately describe his encounter, he simply said, "The pain of my past was taken away so I can be the man I'm supposed to be. I don't know how to explain it any other way. "

Smiling, his three friends watched as he calmly added wood to their fire. Yes, something had definitely changed!

Roany suddenly found himself feeling a little jealous of his friend's new peace and wondered if he was ever going to have a one on one encounter with Chen as all the others had. While the others prepared to go to bed, Roany decided to remain sitting up a little longer as he stared at the stars, occasionally stirring the nearby fire.

Self-pity worked its way into Roany's mind as he pondered the difficult situation he had been forced into. Leaving behind his only living parent was one thing, but realizing that she was the one behind his friend's arrest and the pursuit of the enforcers troubled him greatly. Though he loved Tanzi, he hated what she was doing.

She had always been very aggressive in her pursuit of excellence, for herself and for her family as well. He could still remember his dad as his mother pushed and prodded him to be the top in his profession as a potter. Working tirelessly, until late at night and then leaving early in the morning, Roany hardly knew him.

And then there was his tragic accident when lumberjacks mistakenly toppled a tree in the wrong direction, hitting his father on his way to work. Once he was gone as the focus for his mother's extended perfection, Roany became her main target. It was her unrelenting pressure that first pushed him to accept the apprenticeship position under Jarek, the blacksmith. Once he admitted Galen was right in his observations, Roany finally broke free of her clutches and joined Galen as a dissenter.

Now here he sat, heading towards places still undiscovered with the realization that his own mother had become an enemy of all that he was pursuing…freedom. A wave of sadness suddenly hit him as he pondered both his past and the unknown future that lay before him.

As he sat wallowing in self-pity, he was no longer alone.

"Roany, what are you thinking about?" The unexpected visitor caught him off guard, startling him momentarily.

"Chen! I wasn't expecting to see you!"

"And why not?"

"Oh, you know. With my mother all entangled with the village elders and their pursuit of us, I just figured you wouldn't want much to do with me," he confessed. "My mother is the one who stirred up this whole mess."

"I am very aware of her confusion. And I also can see your struggles with unworthiness," Chen responded. On hearing this, Roany turned towards him, his mind filled with questions. "Don't you realize that my selection of you to make this journey was not based upon how great your upbringing was, who your family is, nor what anyone has done or not done. My choice is based upon who you are."

As the words penetrated his heart, Chen's eyes drew Roany into depths of love that he had never known before.

Betrayal, pressures, and performance melted off of him like snow in a spring rain. As Roany continued looking, he felt warmth penetrating every cell in his body making all things new.

When he finally came to himself, he was sitting alone once again but now feeling very different and free. Every natural sense seemed to be heightened and accentuated as he basked in the lingering love encompassing him.

Eventually, Roany did lie down to rest for a time before the morning sun rose once more, but even as he rested, he found his body and mind more alive than he could ever remember.

Chapter Sixteen

EYES WIDE OPEN

With Oren's recent eye-opening report still running through their heads, Eber and Giza sat across from one another at their table overwhelmed by the information he had shared with them. By the time he had left, night had fallen and even though it was supper time, neither one of them felt like eating.

Candles and lanterns burned around their house creating dancing shadows on the wall that almost appeared to be mocking them as they realized how blind they had been to what was actually going on around them. Giza was the first to break the silence.

"Why didn't we listen to Galen earlier?" she lamented. "He was right all along."

"I guess it's hard to face the truth when our whole lives we have been fed lies and half-truths," Eber admitted.

"Now what are we going to do? We have people watching our house for any sign of Galen and the others so they can be recaptured. Mendi is returning in the morning to help us with splitting wood, but now we know he was sent here only to spy on us and report on our activities. And I liked him!" Giza pointed out. "Now I feel like I have been stabbed in the heart! There's no one left we can trust, except maybe Galen and the other dissenters, and we can't even contact them!"

Tears started to well up in Giza's eyes as Eber glanced over at his grieving wife.

"It was all really my fault," he admitted. "I just didn't want to believe something that devious was going on. I wanted to hang on to my old lifestyle and ignore the warnings we received."

"So what are we going to do?" she asked. "We can't just sit here like bait for our son. We've got to warn him somehow...and I think we need to learn more about the way of the eagle Oren told us about."

"I think you're right. Just sitting here in ignorance is not going to help anyone." Oren agreed. "The first thing we need to do is deal with that deceiver, Mendi, when he returns tomorrow morning."

"And how are we going to do that?"

"Just leave that up to me," Eber advised her. "You just act like everything is normal when he arrives. I think I may have a plan."

"Ok, I guess. I'll do my best not to let on what we now know," she nodded.

"And Giza, for us to break free of all this mess, I have a feeling that we may, at some point, need to leave behind our home. If the enforcers could burn down Oren's home, what would stop them from attempting to do the same to our home? If we want to see Galen, Shoshanna, and the others again, we may need to find a new place to live far from the prying eyes of others. Are you willing to consider this?"

Giza gasped at the idea of leaving their home. This was not something she would have imagined beforehand.

"But where will we go?"

"Honestly, I'm not sure. Maybe there's a chance we can find this Miss Haddie Galen spoke so often about. Or maybe we will run across Oren again and he can give us some direction. All I know is that we cannot remain here much longer. It's too dangerous for both us and Galen. For his sake, we need to move elsewhere. I can build us another home somewhere."

Recognizing Giza was a little shaken by this, Eber allowed his wife a few moments to let this idea sink in.

"Why don't we sleep on this and see if we get any new wisdom in the morning?' he suggested.

"Okay," she agreed.

Slowly the couple rose from their seats extinguishing the candles and lanterns around their home. As the darkness closed in around them, Eber silently cried out to Elemet, the one whom his son and Oren had both mentioned. Though Eber did not really know this Elemet, he realized that the challenges before them were way beyond his own ability to handle. Without a doubt, he needed direction and wisdom to dictate their actions in the days ahead.

With anger still burning inside, Tanzi tromped through the surrounding forest heading for home. Disgusted with the whole group of elders as they dishonored and very nearly rejected any suggestions she made, she considered some options that might change their opinions of her, especially if she came out as the hero in capturing the elusive dissenters. If she was going to turn things around, it was obvious she would need to devise a carefully laid out plan to apprehend the people who knew where the escapees were and maybe even reveal where the Eagles' Nest was located.

She needed to think about that.

Muttering to herself as she walked, Tanzi noticed the trail she was following was growing dimmer. Looking upward through the forest branches, she wondered if an unusually dark cloud had moved in front of the full hazy moon she was dependent upon for additional lighting along with the lantern she was already carrying.

Unable to see any unusual obstructions above her, she held the lantern a little closer to the path so she could continue homeward. Even with the lantern turned up to its highest potential, the light it was emitting persisted in its decreasing illumination until finally Tanzi was forced to stop. She could no longer see where she was going. Darkness enveloped her like a blanket leaving no light at all as a reference point.

Panic set in as she realized without the ability to see, she could not find her way home. Feeling around in desperation, she dropped her lantern grabbing for the first thing she felt...a tree. With both her arms wrapped around its trunk in fear, she desperately fought to find a logical solution to her predicament.

As her heart raced, she stood frozen to the tree afraid to let go lest she encounter something much worse. Wondering what to do, she realized she couldn't stand there clinging to a tree all night. The only thing she could think to do was to cry out for help in the remote chance that someone was walking through the woods at the same time as her.

"Help!" she screamed. "Somebody help me!"

Listening for any kind of response, Tanzi waited, straining her ears for a response.

There was none.

Again she screamed out. "I need help! I can't see!" No response.

One more time, she attempted to be heard.

"Can anyone hear me? I can't see where I am going! I need help!"

As she listened and waited, she could only hear the crickets chirping and frogs croaking in reply. Her heart sank as she stood alone clinging to the tree in complete darkness. Fear eagerly crept in causing every little sound to bring added terror to her mind as she envisioned wolves, bears or even violent criminals attacking and taking advantage of her in this desperate state.

Finally, with no apparent options or answers to her dilemma, hopelessness set in and tears ran down her face as she realized without help, she could be left for days wandering in darkness. She suddenly heard twigs breaking and the crunching of dried leaves as something or someone approached.

A renewed wave of fear washed over her, as she called out hoping that whatever was approaching would, at least, be human, so she could possibly reason with them before they attacked.

"Help! Is someone there? I can't see!"

A male voice answered her in reply. "I'm here. Don't worry. I can assist you home if you like."

"Yes! Yes, please! I can't see anything right now."

"And where do you live?" he asked.

"I live on the outskirts of Kieran," she replied in relief. "I can describe where to go. Thank you so much!" she said reaching out to grab the hand she felt in front of her.

With great care, the man walked her through the forest and with her directions, was able to guide her once again to her home. She could not thank him enough for his kindness! When they finally arrived at her cabin, she invited the stranger to come in for a short time so she could offer him some kind of refreshment in thanks for his assistance.

"No thank you, ma'am," he replied. "I need to return to my own home right now. I can come and check on you in a day or two to see if your vision has returned if you would like."

"Oh, that would be lovely! And please call me, Tanzi," she added. "You never told me your name, sir. What shall I call you?"

"You can just call me 'the woodsman,'" he answered, careful to not reveal his true identity.

"Ok, Mr. Woodsman," she said. "Thank you again for helping me home. I was sure I would be eaten by some creature or wander around until I dropped dead. You have certainly saved my life! Thank you again!"

"You are very welcome, Tanzi. I am leaving now. I'll check on you again soon." With that, the woodsman stepped back outside heading once again into the forest. Once he was a safe distance from Tanzi's house, Oren pulled off his hood smiling as he quickly moved towards Miss Haddie's homestead. He had much to report.

Chapter Seventeen

TIME OF DECISION

"Are you certain it won't hurt him?" Giza asked, a little concerned.

"Look, my family has used this for many generations and not one of us has experienced any side effects from it," Eber consoled her. "Now you understand what you need to be doing while we are gone, right?"

"Yes. I will be ready," Giza promised.

"Ok, so I'm going out to await Mendi's arrival," he responded. With that, Eber stepped out the door to make sure all things on his end were prepared and ready to go.

It was a little later that morning when Mendi arrived, smiling and chipper as always. Eber was the first to greet him.

"Hey there, Mendi!" he called from near his woodpile.

"Good morning!" he replied. "So you have any chores around here that you need some help with today?"

"That is very kind of you to return just to help us again. I hope our needs are not keeping you from your carpentry work," Eber replied in his most virtuous sounding voice. "I certainly wouldn't want you to suffer financially because we are taking up so much of your time."

"Oh, nothing to worry about there. Work is a little slow right now, so I figure I might as well help you while I can."

"That is very kind of you," Eber answered. "So, speaking of your kindness, I have a huge favor to ask of you. Some time back, I cut down a large tree that had some unique rings in the wood that I wanted to integrate into a custom table for Giza and me. The only problem is that it was so large, I had difficulty cutting it up and transporting it here. Would you be willing to help me cut up the tree and help bring the wood back here for me? It would help me out a lot!"

"Sure!" Mendi replied. "It's not too far away, is it?"

"No. It's just a little ways back in the forest. We could have it cut up and back here by lunch."

"Ok. Let's do it!"

"Great!" Eber smiled. "I'll just let Giza know we are leaving and will return soon, then I will grab my cart so we can easily haul it back."

After sticking his head inside the door for a moment, he led Mendi around to the side of the cabin where his hand-pulled cart awaited them along with all the supplies they needed for the short journey that morning. It wasn't long before the two men walked out along one of the many trails leading into the forest.

As they strolled along, the men chatted about a number of things while moving deeper and deeper into the forest.

After a while, Mendi noticed that this was taking longer than he anticipated. When he finally asked Eber about it, Eber acted as though he had lost track of how far they had gone.

"Oh, wait a minute," he said. "I think the tree might just be over there," pointing to their right.

Surprised the fallen tree was not in the vicinity he thought, he circled around a number of times searching for the tree. When he was certain that Mendi was sufficiently disoriented, playing the role of a frustrated and confused old man, Eber suggested they stop, get something to eat and drink to help him get his bearings on exactly where the tree lay.

Producing some light snacks and carefully marked gourds from which to drink, the men sat on the back of the cart as they ate and drank. Suddenly, Mendi was not quite feeling himself. His head was spinning a little and feeling quite tired.

"Oh dear," Eber responded, feigning great concerned for Mendi's well-being. "Hmm. Maybe you should lay down in the back of the cart to rest for a few moments while I take us to the fallen log. I'm sure it is very close by now and I can easily pull you there. You'll probably feel better after a little rest."

The dizziness was not letting up, so Mendi agreed to lay down in the back of the cart for a little while until he felt better. Once Mendi was settled, Eber pulled him along the trail. It wasn't much longer before the young man was completely out and snoring loudly. Eber hummed happily as he hauled the cart and its cargo to a very familiar place where he and his brother had often played when they were boys many years ago.

Back at the cabin, Giza worked feverishly trying to assemble all that they might possibly need for their journey. As she pulled out clothing, provision, and only the most pertinent of items, she found some of her many decisions were rather painful. Not much of all they had accumulated throughout the years would be able to come. She felt as though part of her heart would be left within the walls of their cabin.

As she gathered their items together, Giza reminded herself of Galen and beautiful Shoshanna whom she had grown to love during their short visit so many months ago. She even thought of Roany, her son's childhood friend. Though it was Roany's mother, Tanzi, who had first accused her son of being a dissenter, she couldn't hold that against Roany.

When Roany learned of what had befallen Galen, he was horrified. After Galen and Uri escaped from prison, upon hearing the news, Roany stopped in to check with her and Eber to see if they knew of his whereabouts. When Giza learned Roany was planning to join her son and the others on their journey, she was glad. All they wanted was a place where they would really be free. She couldn't blame any of them!

Once Oren educated them on what was really going on, they quickly realized that keeping their home was not worth the possibility of Galen's recapture. With all this in mind, Giza pushed herself to stay focused, striving to complete the packing before Eber returned, as they had agreed. They would not be used as bait for their own son and his friends!

Several hours later, Eber returned with an empty cart and no Mendi. He came into the cabin laughing a little with a smile on his face.

"How did it go?" Giza asked.

"Perfect! Mendi is sleeping like a baby. By tomorrow morning, he'll wake up wondering where he is and how he got there. "

"Where did you take him, anyway? Somewhere safe, I hope."

"Oh, it is very safe there!" Eber assured her. "My brother and I climbed all through those old caves and even camped out there several times just for fun. They are a little hard to see from the topside, but once you know where to look, they're easy to find."

"I left Mendi with some food, water, blankets, and even an ax in case he needs it," Eber continued. "An ax is rather handy to have if he is forced to set up camp at some point while hiking back home."

"You don't think he could possibly get lost on the way back, do you?" Giza asked, still a little unsure about leaving Mendi the way he did.

"Don't worry, Giza. I also left him a note indicating he needed to travel east so he can eventually find his way back home. Besides, this little adventure will be good for him!" Eber smiled. "It's bound to help make a man out of him rather than the weasel he is. Maybe next time he will think twice before attempting to betraying people who want to become his friends."

Content with Eber's response, Giza once again turned her attention to the task of loading the cart with only their necessary possessions as they prepared to leave behind all that they had once treasured. The cabin which held so many wonderful memories had now become nothing more than a trap for those they loved.

Taking a moment to enjoy their last meal before leaving, Giza tried hard not to look around too long. She ate, but there was a growing lump in her throat as the time for them to leave drew closer. Once finished, Giza automatically began cleaning up the table.

"Giza, you don't have to do that anymore," Eber reminded her. "It's time."

Slowly, Giza brushed her graying brown hair out of her face and followed Eber out the door. Once outside, Eber turned and lit the kindling he had placed next to the exterior of their cabin. As they watched, the fire grew until its flames leaped high enough to reach their newly repaired roof catching it on fire, first. They wanted to make certain that their cabin could never be used as a trap and they could not be used as bait. It was necessary for their home to be utterly destroyed leaving nothing for the village elders to use in the future.

Slowly, the gray-haired man and his wife turned towards one of the paths leading away into the forest where their future was uncertain, to say the least. They only hoped that they would not run into any of the enforcers still searching for the escaped dissenters. Their future now rested entirely in the hands of someone they knew only very little about. Elemet was all they had.

Chapter Eighteen

REPORTING THE NEWS

Miss Haddie and Jessah had been up for some time before Oren knocked on the back door. Rushing over, Jessah opened it and greeting her friend.

"Oren! We were wondering when you would be returning."

"Yes, Oren. Come on in! We are looking forward to hearing how things went for you on your last assignment. Would you like some breakfast?" Miss Haddie asked.

"Yes! A late breakfast sounds wonderful." As Oren walked in and sat down at the table, Jessah and Miss Haddie quickly assembled muffins, fruit, hot tea, and other goodies for their friend. Giving Oren a few moments to eat and sip his sweet tea, the two waited patiently to hear his report.

Finally, after eating his fill, Oren pushed back his chair to relax. No sooner had he done this than Jessah eagerly spoke up.

"Ok. Now tell us what happened on your journey. I can't wait to hear about it!"

Oren laughed at her obvious excitement before continuing.

"Well, I first went to Eber and Giza's cabin to speak with them. I waited until the young man left and then had to step into the "doorway" to avoid being discovered by some enforcers checking the area around their home. Once everything was clear, I went in and spoke with them. I think they received what I had to tell them, though I really don't know what they decided to do."

Miss Haddie spoke up with the information she had.

"I have been informed that they heeded your warning and left their cabin just today. Actually, they decided to burn down the cabin as they left so it could no longer be used as a trap for Galen. I know they will be taken care of. In fact, Oren, I believe you will be meeting up with them again later, directing them where they need to go next."

"Yes, I was sensing that," Oren agreed. "Well, continuing on with my trip, I then ended up in a very unusual late-night meeting where Elemet made sure I was provided with a hooded garb just like everyone else attending. It was just laying outside their meeting hall waiting for me, so I put it on. Once inside, I realized why I was there."

"What was that?" Jessah asked sitting on the edge of her seat barely able to contain herself.

"It was a gathering of village elders from all over the island," Oren explained. "Tanzi, Roany's mother was there giving a report on information she gathered as a result of going through her son's personal things. Some of what she uncovered is not good, I'm afraid."

"And what did she discover?" Miss Haddie inquired.

"She found your name mentioned in his writings and also brought up the Eagles' Nest, though no one knew where that might be. After doing some research on you, she found that your sister, Bina, lives in Chana. When she mentioned that Bina was blind and quite elderly, the others pretty much scoffed at her suggestion to have enforcers watch Ms. Bina's cabin, just in case any of us showed up."

"At that point," Oren continued, "Tanzi was asked to leave, and I heard Elemet instructing me to follow her into the woods. It's a good thing I did, as blindness suddenly came upon her. I was able to lead her back home, without revealing my name, of course. I did tell her that I would check on her in a couple of days to see how she was coming along. She was very grateful."

Excitedly, Jessah had to ask, "So who did you say you were if you didn't tell her your name?"

"I told her she could just call me 'the woodsman,'" he replied.

"The Woodsman," Miss Haddie repeated. "I like that. Maybe we can use that as your nickname when you are out on your assignments. Wonderful! So, in regards to my name being mentioned and Bina's location revealed, we may need to do something to protect my sister further in the days ahead. Right now, however, I believe her blindness is actually something that can work to her advantage. As you already know, I am quite safe where I am, but we must use caution so as to not draw any further attention to Bina and Yona."

"Does that mean I won't be able to visit them anymore?" Jessah asked, a little distressed.

"I'm not entirely certain what changes that might mean for us, but there is nothing to worry about, child," Miss Haddie replied. "Elemet is aware of it all, and he will direct us as things progress. However, I am aware of a new assignment coming up for you, Jessah, that I know will excite you."

"Really?"

"Yes, but first I need to train you in another way of moving around on the island. You will like this."

Beaming, Jessah nearly jumped up and down in excitement. "Oh, I can't wait!"

Turning her attention back to Oren, Miss Haddie encouraged him to rest up the remainder of the day so he was refreshed for his next journey. Oren wholeheartedly agreed and exited out the back door to his own place. Once Oren left, Jessah was right at Miss Haddie's side. "So when do we begin?"

Smiling, Miss Haddie picked up a few of the dishes left behind by Oren and encouraged Jessah to do the same. "Let's start by cleaning up first, and then we'll learn about traveling, okay?"

"Yes, ma'am!" Jessah jumped up and joined Miss Haddie in cleaning up before the real lessons began.

Meanwhile, Eber and Giza wandered down one of the forest trails, quite unsure as to where they were going. The older couple grew weary after going what seemed to be a relatively short distance from their burning cabin. Part of their weariness was based upon all the morning's activity and part was the grief of leaving everything behind as they moved towards their new and unknown destiny. Finally, Eber could hold his peace no longer.

"Giza, I have something to tell you that I am not proud about."

Immediately concern came over her face as Giza looked at her husband.

"What is it?"

"You know how I told you I left instructions for Mendi telling him how to get back home?"

"Yes," she replied.

"Well, my instructions were not entirely true."

"What do you mean?"

"When I told Mendi to head east so he could find his way back home, it actually should have said northeast," he said bowing his head a little.

Giza stared at him momentarily before laughing out loud in relief. She had thought it might have been much more serious than that.

"So, where did you direct him to go?" she asked, still giggling a little.

"Well, if he just goes east, he will eventually come to the ocean," Eber replied.

"I guess he really will be learning a good many lessons through that," Giza smiled.

While they were still discussing Mendi, Eber happened to notice a light coming out of the darkened forest ahead. Not wanting to expose Giza to any danger, he immediately had both her and their cart safely tucked out of sight, while he proceeded to explore what lay before them.

Drawing closer to the light, Eber peered out from behind a large tree. Sitting before him was a blazing campfire with plenty of food and even a tent already set up. A lone man sat on a fallen log heating up water for the tea he was about to prepare. Before even glancing up into his direction, the man called out.

"Eber! Welcome! I have been expecting you and Giza. Would you like to join me for supper?" he asked.

Immediately suspecting the man to be in league with the village elders and their enforcers, Eber politely declined the man's offer thinking it might be a trap. Without Eber even voicing any of his suspicions, the man answered them.

"No, I am not working with the village elders nor the enforcers," he assured him. "I am actually from the Eagles' Nest where your son is heading right now."

This caught Eber's attention. The man continued.

"I know that you and Giza must be tired, especially after the ordeal of walking away from all that you own. Elemet and I are so pleased with your decision and wanted to assure you that you both will be well taken care of. You have nothing to fear."

Eber's eyes grew wide at the mention of Elemet's name. He had not even told Giza that he had asked Elemet for help!

"Who are you?" Eber inquired.

"My name is Chen and I work very closely with Elemet in all that is going on," he explained. "In fact, not that long ago I sat with your son, Galen, and we had a wonderful talk as well. Let me assure you, he and all his friends are doing admirably." Chen allowed all this new information to soak in before encouraging Eber to go and fetch Giza.

Once Giza and the cart had been pulled next to the campsite, Eber introduced Chen to his wife.

"Can you tell her what you told me about Galen and the others?" Eber asked wanting Giza to hear the good news firsthand.

Once they were filled in on the progression of their son towards the Eagles' Nest, Chen invited the couple to eat and relax while he helped them further understand the battle they had found themselves in. While sipping the warm, spicy tea, Chen spoke and shared many things with them as they grew warm and filled with the goodness and favor of Elemet.

It was quite late before Chen concluded his brief history of all that had transpired on the island of Kumani. Even though their bodies were tired, the couple soaked in the truth hungrily until finally, Chen encouraged them to retire for the evening.

"But will we be safe here?" Eber asked. "What if the enforcers search this part of the forest tonight or even tomorrow morning? They may discover our location."

"Not to fear, my dear Eber," Chen replied. "You are farther away than you think and you are more protected than you realize."

With that, Chen looked up to the treetops above. Suddenly Eber and Giza realized the trees around them swelled in size creating an impenetrable hedge of safety for them. Their mouths dropped open in amazement, but they were even further surprised when Chen, after saying goodnight, stepped right through the trees and vanished from sight.

As the couple crawled into their comfortable tent for the evening, a sweet peace washed over them allowing sleep to come upon them quickly as they dreamed of the beautiful new future now emerging before them.

Chapter Nineteen

AN UNEXPECTED VISIT

Sometime after breakfast, Ms. Bina heard a knock at her door. The sound startled both Ms. Bina and Yona who was cleaning up in the kitchen. Drying her hands off, Yona assured Ms. Bina that she would see who was at the door.

When she opened the door, a young man stood before her. At first, he just stood and gazed at the lovely young girl opening the door. Distracted by her piercing dark eyes and flowing brown hair cascading around her face, he found Yona quite stunning. Yona was beginning to feel a little annoyed at this interruption when he finally came to himself, recalling the purpose of his visit that morning.

"Hi! My name is Zelig. And what was your name?"

"My name is Yona. Can I help you with something?" she asked, rather irritated at this point. This young man did look somewhat familiar, but she couldn't quite place where she had seen him before.

"Yes, Yona. I was wondering if Ms. Bina was at home."

"Yes, she is here. Why do you ask?" Yona inquired, feeling a little protective of the sweet, older woman she had grown to love.

"Well, I have been sent to check on all our older residents to make sure they are being taken care of sufficiently," Zelig explained, even as his eyes continued studying the young girl. "May I come in and speak with her?" Growing uncomfortable with his continued stares, Yona looked back over her shoulder to see if Ms. Bina was willing. Secretly she hoped she would be allowed to slam the door in his face, but he was asking for Ms. Bina.

"Yes, Yona," she called out. "You can let Zelig come in."

"Come on in," Yona said reluctantly. As Zelig entered the home, he took a quick look around before following Yona to the chair where Ms. Bina sat. "Ms. Bina, this is Zelig."

Ms. Bina extended her hand out to greet the man. After their greeting, the elderly woman encouraged him to sit so they could talk. It wasn't often that they had visitors from her village and she was curious to see what this was about.

"Ms. Bina, I have been sent here to check on your well-being. We know you are getting older and just wanted to make certain you were receiving all the care you needed," he began.

Sensing that Yona was nearby, Ms. Bina encouraged her to pull up a chair and sit next to her before attempting to answer Zelig. Once Yona was seated, Ms. Bina reached out for her hand and held it before responding to their visitor's questions.

"Oh, I am just fine," Ms. Bina replied. "As you can see, Yona is taking wonderful care of me. Thank you for checking," she answered with a smile.

"How is your health holding up?"

"Well, as you can see, I am blind, but Yona keeps me informed on what is going on when I need to know."

"So, are you pretty much alone most of the time, besides Yona, of course, or are you able to have sufficient social interaction with any other people?"

"Oh, I am quite satisfied with Yona and the few neighbors who do knock on my door from time to time," she replied. "Thank you for asking."

"What about family? Do you have any family members nearby who check in on you?" he asked with raised eyebrows.

"Well, unfortunately, my husband and I had no children and any other family members are now long gone."

"Oh!" he replied while searching for anything else he could ask about. "I guess that is all I need to know for now. Thank you for answering my questions. I will be sure to report that you are well taken care of to the village elders. I must be leaving now. Goodbye Ms. Bina," he added while standing to his feet. Before he stepped out the door, he gave Yona one more look over after she walked him to the door, grateful that she could finally shut the door behind him. As soon as he left, Ms. Bina spoke up.

"That snake!" she said.

"Why do you say that? Did you sense something as well?" Yona asked. "He made me feel so uncomfortable!"

"Once I shook his hand, I saw him being sent out by the village elders to attempt to collect information about my sister."

"You saw that? How is that possible?"

"Do you remember how I was able to see things when I held Jessah's hands and yours as well?" Ms. Bina reminded her.

"Oh yes!"

"Well, now I am getting pictures just by holding someone's hand briefly. Also, when I was holding your hand while he was speaking, I could clearly see him sitting before me."

"That is amazing! Well, we can certainly put that to good use any time you need to see something," Yona responded.

"Yes, that can be very handy right now," she agreed. "I will need to tell Haddie all about this the next time she visits. We don't need any enforcers snooping around my home."

"That's true, especially if we have any visiting friends like Jessah. That would be awful to have someone check on us while she was here!" Yona reminded her. "Oh, and I was curious about one of the answers you gave Zelig. You said all your family members were now long gone. What about Miss Haddie?"

"Well, though I saw Haddie several nights ago, she is now long gone. Right?" Ms. Bina said with a smile.

"Oh, I get it!" Yona said, laughing.

"I really need to speak with Haddie so she can give me some wisdom on how to handle these types of intrusions. She will know what we should do."

"Oh, I just remembered where I have seen Zelig before!" Yona recalled. "He was the one making the announcement regarding new enforcers when I went to the marketplace in the village!"

"Hmm," Ms. Bina responded. "I wonder how involved this Zelig is with the village elders. We will have to use caution if he shows up again. That is for sure!"

Zelig walked briskly through the village square to his father's print shop where he worked. As he burst through the doors, he immediately announced to his father what he had learned by visiting Ms. Bina's home.

"Ms. Bina is just a blind old lady who knows nothing," Zelig blurted out, "however, there is a beautiful young lady working for her. I think she is the one I want to have as my wife."

"Okay, son. Stay focused on what you were sent to do. Did you find out if she has a sister?" Cobar pressed him.

"She said all of her family members were long gone. She's the only one left now."

"I knew it! That Tanzi was giving us inaccurate information at the meeting!" Cobar responded.

"But what about that girl I want? Can you get her for me?" Zelig persisted.

"One thing at a time. First, did you get her name?"

"Yes. Her name is Yona, and she is beautiful."

"Yona? Okay, let me check in the book of records," he said while pulling out a large well-worn book and placing it on the table before them. Zelig stared over his shoulder as his father ran his finger through all the names beginning with the letter "Y." "Let's see. Yakira, Yatva, Yitta. Oh, here it is! Yona." Silently he read to himself until Zelig could stand no more.

"So what does it say about her?" he demanded.

"This says that she is an orphan from Camp Shabelle. When it was reported that Ms. Bina went blind and needed some help, I contacted Miss Moselle, director of the training center and Yona was sent over. Hmm. It says she is only twelve years old, though."

"But she looks so much older! Twelve is old enough, isn't it? I really want her!" Zelig insisted.

"Well, being as she is an orphan, there really isn't anyone who could object to her name being added to our list of available young women. We could just order a new orphan from Camp Shabelle for Ms. Bina when that time came, I guess. Besides, with Ms. Bina being so old, she probably won't last that long anyway." his father reasoned.

"Yes, yes! Put Yona's name on the list and then you can make sure that she is given to me, right?"

"Yes, I can take care of that for you," Cobar replied. "You know, you have quite a heritage before you," he reminded his son as he opened the closet door pointing to his hooded garb used at all the gatherings of the village elders. "If you stay the course, someday you, too, can have the great privilege of deciding how things should go on this island. With our identity protected, the people really have no idea which of their neighbors is actually running their lives. We get to tell young men where they will work, inform young women who will be their husbands, and then deal with any dissenters. It's really quite an honor."

"Yes, I know that father. I just want to make sure I get Yona at the next presentation of available women," Zelig stressed to his father.

"Don't you worry. The list of young women will be going out shortly and Yona will be notified to begin preparing for her presentation. With her already taking care of Ms. Bina, it looks like she will have plenty of experience in running a home for you. This should work out just fine," he concluded.

Zelig smiled in anticipation. "I can't wait!"

Chapter Twenty

HOME SWEET HOME

As Eber and Giza climbed out of their tent, refreshed and invigorated by both the rest and the many wonderful dreams they each had, they were surprised to see Oren sitting at their campfire with hot tea already prepared for them to enjoy.

"Good morning, my friends," Oren greeted them. "Did you sleep well?"

"Best sleep I can remember in a long time!" Eber responded as he headed over to join Oren next to the warm fire.

"Did you sleep well, also Ms. Giza?" Oren asked.

"I felt like I was floating on a cloud all night!" she answered as she sat next to her husband. Suddenly she noticed the trees around them were back to their original shapes and no longer creating the barrier around them. "Look, Eber! The trees are back to normal!"

"Oh, so they are! That was quite impressive when Chen caused the tree to swell up and protect us last night. He is something else!"

"Yes," Oren responded. "I'm sure he is. I can't wait until I meet him in person myself."

"Eber, do you remember his eyes?" Giza added and then speaking to Oren, she said, "Did you know he has beautiful swirling blue eyes that just suck you in?"

"I have heard that," Oren replied. "I'm sure I will see for myself one day soon. So, are you both ready for your next adventure?"

"Well, maybe," Eber said, "As long as I get a chance to enjoy my breakfast."

"Of course! Both of you go ahead and eat. While you get your fill, maybe I can explain what Elemet has planned for you, as long as you agree."

"Yes, please go on," Giza encouraged him. "I'm sure Elemet has nothing but good intended for us old folks."

"Who are you calling old?" Eber retorted with a smile. "I prefer being called "well cured." We might be a little wrinkled up, but our value is still preserved."

After a good laugh, the couple proceeded to eat as Oren spoke.

"Once, breakfast is done, I will help you pack up so we can continue our way to your new home."

"A new home?" Giza cried out in amazement. "You mean Eber doesn't have to build us a home? I am so relieved!"

Turning towards his wife, Eber questioned her response. "Are you relieved that we have a home or that I am not the one building a home for you?"

"Well, it's not that I don't appreciate all your efforts, but with us being a little 'well cured,' you have to admit it would take you a lot longer to finish a project like that. Right? I just didn't want to be homeless for an extended period of time, that's all."

Eber had to agree having a house already prepared for them was much better than him trying to build one. Oren then continued describing the plans Elemet had for the couple.

"Elemet is asking if you would be willing to serve as a safe haven for any dissenters heading towards the smoking mountains. He would cause your homestead to become much like what Miss Haddie now has," he explained. "You will find that, just like you saw happen with the forest protecting you as you slept, in the same manner, the forest will keep you safe and protected should someone come wandering around your area, unless they are led by the light as so many of us have been in the past."

"That is a huge relief," Eber commented. Oren continued his explanation of what was to come.

"You will soon find that I may be one of your regular guests as I roam through these woods helping people from time to time. This will make it a much shorter journey for me than to return to Miss Haddie's every time. I have also learned that I am to further instruct you in the ways of the eagle each time I come through. Basically, I will be teaching you whatever I am learning as well."

"And you will be more than welcome at any time," Giza chimed in. "We would greatly enjoy seeing you on a regular basis and would appreciate any instruction you can offer us. This is all so new!"

Seeing that they were nearly done with their breakfast, Oren encouraged them to begin packing things up so they could begin their journey to their new home. It didn't take them long to get everything ready. With Oren and Eber pulling their cart together, the journey actually took a relatively short time and when they saw their new home, Giza was more than thrilled. Eber, impressed with the workmanship, was equally satisfied. Once the couple settled in, Oren took his leave and headed for his next assignment; checking in on Tanzi.

Miss Haddie had assured him, she would still be without her sight when he arrived, so his identity would be protected. Whether or not, he would reveal whom he was depended entirely upon how Tanzi was responding to her world of darkness.

Oren moved with great caution keeping a sharp eye open for any enforcers combing through the forest, as he now knew his name and sketches of him had been circulated throughout the villages offering a generous bounty for his capture. As he drew closer to Tanzi's cabin, he slowed his pace and took the time to listen for any further instructions coming from Elemet.

Without any new information, Oren moved closer to the front door and decided to knock.

"Who's there?" Tanzi asked.

"It's me, the woodsman, returning to check on you as I promised."

"Oh, come it!" she called out. "I was hoping you might return." Cracking open the door, Oren first peeked in to see where Tanzi might be. As he scanned the entryway, he noticed her sitting alone at her table with not just one cup of tea sitting in front of her, but two different cups.

Sensing his hesitation, Tanzi encouraged him, "Don't worry. I am all alone now."

Stepping into the cabin, Oren took a moment to look all around in case someone was in hiding, but as she had said, she was alone.

"It looks like you had some company earlier," he commented as he approached the table.

"I did, but I don't think it was anyone you would object to."

"Why is that?" Oren asked, his curiosity piqued.

"Not long ago, I was visited by someone named Chen. He told me you would be coming soon."

"He did? What else did he tell you?"

"We spoke for quite a long time and he explained how I had been fooled into believing a great many things that were not true."

"Really!" Feeling much better about his visit, Oren asked if he might prepare some more tea for both of them before he sat down.

"Oh yes, please. That would be lovely. However, before you decide to join me, I must tell you something."

"Go ahead. I'm listening."

"I need you to know that I am the one who got this whole mess stirred up by reporting Galen and having him arrested."

"Yes, I heard that," Oren responded while pouring the tea.

"I am also the one who reported Shoshanna as one of the dissenters."

Oren walked over to the table with two cups of hot tea, placing one directly in front of Tanzi. Reaching over, he guided her hand to the cup so she could drink.

"Thank you," she responded before continuing. "And now I must tell you, I am also the one who inspired the enforcers to burn down your cabin. I had the village elders add your name to the list of dissenters along with the others and then place a bounty on your head," she said even as a tear dripped down her cheek. "I now realize how I have caused much pain and suffering in the lives of many people, including my own son!"

Oren said nothing but continued staring at the woman wondering if he really heard her correctly.

"If you cannot stay, Oren. I understand. I will not mention your name to anyone else should they come by, but I wanted you to know how sorry I am. Would you ever be able to forgive me?"

"So, what are you saying? Not even two nights ago, I heard you telling the village elders the names of people that I care about and asking them to investigate a sweet old lady who is also blind. Have you changed your mind about all that as well?"

"I was unable to change my mind until I saw the depths of darkness I had allowed to control me. While sitting with Chen, he told me things I had never heard before. I can't really explain it, but as he spoke to the depths of my despair, things broke off, and, though I am still blind, I am beginning to see for the very first time," she explained.

"I saw how all my striving for success had actually driven the ones I loved away from me. Roany is now gone, and I can't blame him in the least. I don't know what will happen in the future, but I do know that I am no longer in league with the village elders and their plots. I came to a decision to embrace the truth and even invited Elemet to direct my miserable life as he chooses."

"Chen did tell me," she continued, "that if you chose to do so, you might lay your hands upon my eyes for me to see. If you decide not to, I will accept my blindness and do whatever little I can to help protect the dissenters in the days ahead. It is up to you, for I have greatly offended both you and many others by my hatred and blindness."

With her head bowed, Tanzi waited for Oren's decision.

The room was silent for some time causing Tanzi to even wonder if Oren had silently slipped out. Just as she was coming to that place of accepting the man's decision, she felt his hands positioned upon her eyes. She cried as he silently called upon Elemet to restore her sight.

After a short time his hands lifted off and Tanzi looked upon the man to whom she had caused much loss and sorrow for the first time.

Oren smiled at her. At that moment, she knew things would now drastically change for her in the days ahead.

The two sat and talked for quite some time as they wondered how Elemet was going to direct her in this new life of freedom, especially with so many village elders knowing who she was and how much she knew about them.

Her life was entirely in Elemet's hands at that point.

Chapter Twenty-One

FACING FEARS

The weary travelers continued to slowly progress on the serpentine trails of the mountains before them. Several days had passed since their time of refreshing found in the mountain meadow. With weary bodies once again, they found themselves fighting the temptation to stop even though they knew they must proceed.

"How are you doing, Shoshanna?" Galen asked as he noticed her breathing a little hard as they walked.

"Well, I wouldn't mind having a lunch break, if that is what you are asking me. I know we haven't been walking that long, but it feels like I've been walking all night!" she admitted.

"How about you two? Are you ready to take a break as well?"

"Well, if food is involved with the break, then I am all in," Uri responded.

"Sure. I would definitely enjoy a break myself," Roany added.

"Ok. Let's keep our eyes open for a good spot to take a lunch break," Galen agreed.

After some discussion, the group decided to press on just beyond the next crest of the trail, so when they stopped, they could take a look at what lay before them as they rested. Once they reached the top, instead of looking at the beautiful glades and meadows they were accustomed to seeing in the distance, they saw what appeared to be a massive forest fire raging through the trees ahead. All four stood in silence as they could hardly believe their eyes. This was not what they were expecting at all!

Thoughts of discouragement and fear swept over them. How in the world could they possibly travel through a blazing forest to reach the Eagles' Nest? Could this actually be part of the plan?

Realizing that fear was taking ahold of them, Galen encouraged his friends to just focus on getting things set up for a quick lunch break before moving on. None of them was sure, however, if progressing much further was even possible. As they unloaded their knapsacks, pulling out the remaining food from their previous feast, they couldn't help but glance up with some trepidation from time to time.

As they slowly ate, Roany happened to take a closer look at the fiery timbers blocking their way just beyond the next bluff. Suddenly something caught his attention. Standing up, he took a closer look at the blaze.

"Hey! Look at that!" he exclaimed. The others immediately joined him studying the burning forest ahead. "Check out the tops of the trees! They don't appear to be charred at all. The branches look green and completely undamaged by the flames!"

"Yes! I can see that!" Shoshanna concurred. "Maybe this fire is not what it appears to be at all." Uri kept looking, but still wasn't fully convinced.

"I keep thinking back to some of the instructions Chen has given us," Galen added. "Remember what he said about peripheral things? He told us not to be distracted by them."

"I wouldn't exactly call this a peripheral item," Uri responded. "It's pretty much right in front of us!"

"Yes, but remember, our main task was to follow the trail leading to the Eagles' Nest and anything else is just a peripheral item as far as our focus right now. Isn't that true?" Galen responded.

"I think you are right," Shoshanna added. "I think if we only focus on what we've been told to do, any obvious hindrances must yield."

"This might just be an illusion created to discourage us from our goal," Roany said.

"Or it could also be something created to test our resolve in following through," Galen suggested. "I say we pack up and head directly towards the fire."

"Well, I suppose if all of you are prepared to become a toasted offering in order to demonstrate your willingness to follow directions, I guess I am willing, too," Uri commented. "Though, walking through flames is not something I am looking forward to."

"All right then," Galen called out. "Let's do this!" As the four friends loaded up their knapsacks, Galen moved over near Shoshanna and quietly whispered into her ear. "In case no one has ever told you before, I think you are the bravest woman I have ever met. I hope after we arrive at the Eagles' Nest that we might have more time to really get to know each other without all these pressures and challenges we are constantly facing."

Shoshanna looked into his eyes, quite surprised by his admiration. She too was attracted by Galen's ability to take the lead in such a difficult journey.

"I would enjoy that myself," she responded with a slight blush. Nodding, Galen stepped away to spearhead their journey back onto the trail leading directly into the fiery forest.

Perspiration broke out on the brows of each traveler as they moved closer and closer to the flames completely engulfing the trees. They could feel the temperature rising as both their clothing and faces grew quite warm. Finally, they reached the place of no return where they were left with the option of turning back or stepping into the inferno.

Galen, looking back at his three friends, swallowed to try and moisten his dry throat. He had to be the first one to set the example. His heart knew what he needed to do, but logic and the radiant heat all over his body were screaming at him to abandon this "foolish plan." He had come too far to abandon his confidence at this point.

Taking one final breath, he stepped into the flames and then vanished in front of the others. The three remaining friends listened for any screams of pain and heard none. Shoshanna was next to take the plunge and stepped forward with her eyes closed into the fiery inferno. She also disappeared. Neither Roany nor Uri wanted to be left behind, so they followed their friends into the flames while holding their breaths and closing their eyes.

Once on the other side of the fiery curtain, the four travelers were in awe of the peace and beauty that flooded the mountain pass paradise they had stepped into. Birds twittered happily all around them as pillars of light penetrated the shadows of the forest with sparkling particles dancing all around them. Cool breezes immediately relieved the heat coming from the flames behind them. The illusion of fire had been a test of their resolve. Gratefully, they moved ahead, refreshed by their obedience.

The afternoon passed with no further difficulties until they arrived at what appeared to be a narrow canyon with a trail requiring them to walk single file through it. Rather than tackle a whole new challenge, Galen and the others decided it might be time to set up camp for the night allowing them to negotiate the canyon trail after a full night of sleep.

A fire was built and tents were set up before the night darkness set in. After finishing the last of their food, the friends sat upon fallen logs enjoying the peaceful sounds of the night. Far in the distance, they could hear the howling of wolves as they gazed at the bright moon above. Crickets sang in chorus with the leaves above them rustling in the gentle breezes.

The fire crackled and popped before them even as they heard the flapping of wings far above them. Thinking it was only owls on the hunt for small vermin, the four eventually headed into their tents and without any delay, entered into a well-deserved sleep.

Chapter Twenty-Two

LOST AND FOUND

Weak with hunger, Mendi finally found his way back to the village of Kieran and headed directly back to Eber and Giza's home only to find it a ruined ash heap of burnt timbers. He had planned on confronting them, but with the cabin gone, he instead headed over to Tanzi's home to report what had happened to him.

Quietly sipping a cup of tea, Tanzi was surprised to have a visitor so early in the morning and was equally shocked when she saw a bedraggled and exhausted Mendi standing before her.

"What have you been doing, Mendi?" she asked. "You look like you have been wrestling a bear!"

"Well, in one sense I was! Could I please just come in? I am so tired!"

"Oh yes! Come in, please! Can I get you anything?" she asked.

"How about something to eat, something to drink, and some new clothes? I can't possibly explain everything I have been through in the last couple of days!" he whined. "I'll bet you were concerned about me when I didn't show up to make my report, right?"

Not wanting to let on she hadn't even noticed, Tanzi just smiled saying, "Actually, I have been rather preoccupied myself these last couple of days. However, I am ready to hear your report now!" As Mendi stumbled in, Tanzi brought him some of Roany's old clothing to change into and prepared some hot tea for him to sip while she brought out some fruit, biscuits, and cheese. Once his needs were taken care of, Tanzi encouraged him to share his tale of woe.

"Well, first when I arrived at Eber and Giza's home to help them as I had in the past, Eber took me on this wild goose chase in the woods looking for some fallen tree he needed help loading. When we couldn't find it, we decided to take a break to eat something before continuing. I was sipping some kind of strange tea when I suddenly felt funny," Mendi explained.

"Eber encouraged me to lay down to rest in his cart while he looked for that fallen tree again. When I woke up, I was in a cave, left only with a few basic things and directions telling me to go east so I could find my way back here. Well, let me tell you, those directions were wrong!" Mendi took another sip of his tea and a bite of his biscuit before continuing as Tanzi worked hard not to crack a smile. Eber and Giza had certainly outsmarted him!

"I don't know how, but I eventually found my way back, and when I went to confront Eber and Giza, they were gone and their cabin was burnt to the ground! What is going on here?" he demanded. "Do you know where they have gone and why their cabin was destroyed?"

"No Mendi, I don't know what happened or where they have gone, but I am glad you found your way back here," she said, trying to cheer him up a little. "Did you have a difficult time in the woods?"

"I've never been much of an outdoorsman," he admitted, "and now I know for sure that I have no intention of becoming one, either! That was rough! I mean really rough out there!"

"I am so sorry for you," she said trying to appear sympathetic. "Well, it looks like your assignment is over and now you can just go back to whatever you were doing before, I suppose."

"No, I think I'm going to continue working with the village elders. Now I'm even more eager to catch those dissenters trying to ruin our way of life, but it certainly won't be by dragging myself through the woods!" he lamented. "I need a nice, safe, indoor assignment where I can just observe someone who isn't traipsing through the woods for no reason at all. I need to discuss this with the village elders to see if they can find me an easier job."

"Well, good luck with that, Mendi," Tanzi said. "I hope they can accommodate your needs."

After Mendi left, Tanzi had to smile again at the wisdom Eber had shown in dealing with the elders' chosen spy. As she sat down again, she mulled over Oren's advice to just lay low and not let on that she had, in fact, become a dissenter herself. He was going to check with Miss Haddie to see what wisdom she had to offer for someone in Tanzi's precarious position.

All she could do was wait and see what transpired.

Meanwhile, it was time for Yona to head into the marketplace again for her weekly shopping for Ms. Bina. Everything was calm and normal in the village of Chana, not like before when new enforcers were being recruited. That was a relief as she was easily able to cross the village square in search of the supplies they were running low on.

As she passed by the wall used for announcements, she noticed a new paper posted. Curious, she wandered over to see what it said. The announcement had to do with available young women selected for presentation to the eligible young men the following month. Nothing for her to be concerned with. Just to see if she knew anyone on the list, she started glancing down. When she came to the "Y" section, her mouth dropped open and she very nearly released everything she was holding to the ground.

"Yona?" she read to herself. Couldn't be! She was only 12 years old! Someone must have made a mistake. Before she went any further, she decided to enter the print shop where the lists were created.

Pushing the door open, Yona boldly asked to speak with whoever was in charge. Standing up from his desk and the chair behind the counter, Cobar stepped up to the unflinching young woman before him.

"May I help you?" he said as he looked her over.

"That list posted outside," she began. "There must be some mistake. My name is on that list and I am only twelve years old! I'm not ready for marriage!" Feigning a little surprise, he picked up another copy of the list and looked it over.

"Let me check. What is your name, miss?"

"My name is Yona."

"Well, let's see what we have here," he replied knowing full well his son's intentions for her.

"Oh yes! Why there you are, my dear. Yona," he said with a forced smile. "Congratulations, Yona! In a month you will have the opportunity to settle into your own home with a brand new husband!"

"But I don't want a husband right now! I am taking care of Ms. Bina who is blind. I cannot get married now," she insisted.

"Well, unfortunately, my dear, the elders have made their decision. There must be a surplus of eligible bachelors for them to include you for this next presentation process."

"But what about Ms. Bina? She needs me!" Yona objected again.

"Not to worry, Yona. There are plenty of other orphans to replace you at Ms. Bina's," he reminded her. "The good news is it appears as if your care for Ms. Bina has helped prepare you for marriage. Congratulations again!"

"No! This can't be right!" she said as a tear slipped down her cheek. "Is there anyone else I can speak to about this?"

"No. I'm afraid the decision has already been made for the good of all and the necessary survival for all of us here on Kumani. You know that," he added with a smirk. "I guess the village elders will be seeing you in a month, my dear."

Angrily, Yona turned around and stormed out the door. In no way and in no manner did she intend to marry someone village elders chose for her! Rather than continuing with her shopping, Yona headed home to inform Ms. Bina of what had transpired. They needed help, and soon!

Shortly after Yona, stepped out of the print shop, Zelig appeared from behind a back door smiling.

"Didn't I tell you she was a looker?"

"That she is, indeed," Cobar agreed. "She also has a bit of spunk you will need to deal with, I see."

"Oh, that won't be a problem for me!" he assured his father. "I can handle her." Nodding, Cobar returned to his desk while Zelig dreamed about the day when Yona would be his.

Chapter Twenty-Three

A NEW WAY

"So I won't be flying on the back of Goldie anymore?" Jessah asked, a little concerned.

"Goldie? Who is Goldie?" Miss Haddie inquired.

"Goldie is the nickname I have given the golden eagle I have ridden on. He seems to like it," she added with a smile.

"Well child, you may still ride on the eagle from time to time, but this new assignment must be accomplished at night."

"You mean I get to go out alone at night? That sounds exciting!"

"Actually, you won't have to go out as much as you will just be moved to the place where Elemet needs you, and then he will bring you back here," Miss Haddie explained.

"Oh, you mean like when you visited your sister?"

"Yes. That's right. Just like that."

"So, where will Elemet be sending me?" she asked.

"Oh, it is a very special assignment, perfect for someone like you!" Miss Haddie replied.

Just then a knock was heard on their back door. They both immediately knew who it was.

"Oren is back and up already?" Jessah commented. "I'm looking forward to hearing about all his travels these last days."

"I am, too," Miss Haddie agreed. "Would you mind letting him in, Jessah?"

Jessah hurried over and opened the door for their friend. As soon as he entered, she cheerfully greeted him.

"Good morning, Oren!"

"Well, good morning to you, Jessah!" he said while bending down to look her in the eye. "You are certainly a chipper young lady this morning!"

"I'm excited because Miss Haddie is going to tell me about my new very special assignment!"

"Oh really? I'd love to hear about this as well. May I join you?" he asked, still looking at Jessah.

"Of course you can!" she responded, looking in Miss Haddie's direction. With Miss Haddie's nod of approval, Jessah grabbed Oren's hand and led him over to join them at the table.

"Before we start, maybe we can offer Oren some hot tea and biscuits for his breakfast," Miss Haddie suggested. Eagerly, Jessah ran over to grab some fresh biscuits and honey for their guest while Miss Haddie brought over the tea for him to enjoy. Once everything was in place, Jessah quickly sat down again in her chair and prepared to hear about Elemet's plans for her. Miss Haddie continued as Oren listened while sipping his tea.

"So, have you thought much about that awful Camp Shabelle since you left there?"

"Actually, I have not thought too much about it since Yona and I are no longer there," Jessah admitted.

"Well, Elemet has not forgotten that place and all the orphans forced to endure Miss Moselle and all the indoctrination they teach there."

"What does 'indoctrination' mean?" she asked. Looking towards Oren, Miss Haddie invited Oren to explain the word to her.

"Hmm. I would say that 'indoctrination' is where people teach someone just what they want to tell them, whether it is true or not. Do you understand that?" Oren asked Jessah.

"I think so. You are saying that the lessons taught to the orphans at Camp Shabelle are not true. Right?"

"Yes. Exactly," he responded. Miss Haddie then continued addressing Jessah herself.

"So, as you remember, lots of things taught at Camp Shabelle were designed to keep the children under the control of the village elders when they leave the school, and you know that is not right. Yes?"

"Oh yes! I learned to just ignore whatever they were saying during my lessons."

"Good! You learned about Elemet early on and were able to recognize what was true and what was not, but what about all those children who have not yet heard about Elemet and the way of the eagle? No one has told them about that yet."

"That is true," Jessah replied. "So Elemet wants to take me at night to speak with the children there? Right?"

"Yes! Exactly," Miss Haddie responded. "He wants to take you from time to time to help teach the children what is actually true, and then he will bring you back here. How does that sound?"

"It sounds absolutely amazing!"

"I thought you might like that," Miss Haddie smiled. "We can talk some more about when this will start and the things you need to share with the children you visit. Okay?"

"Okay!" Jessah replied as her eyes sparkled in excitement. Turning her attention to Oren, Miss Haddie encouraged him to give his report of all that had happened with the placement of Eber and Giza in their new protected homestead and his visit with Tanzi.

As Oren described his travels and the beautiful transformation in Tanzi since Chen's visit, Jessah sat with her head resting upon her folded arms on the table. She was in awe of how Elemet was working so beautifully in orchestrating the lives of his people. Oren continued.

"So the thing we need to discuss and seek wisdom on is what to do with Tanzi. She is willing to stay where she is at for the moment, but there certainly will be a time when the village elders will begin asking questions. Her life might be in danger if she is identified as a dissenter. She knows far too much about the operations of the village elders and their schemes. We need to discuss what might be best for her safety soon."

"Yes, I totally agree, Oren. Let's see if Elemet gives us any wisdom as to where she needs to go in the future."

"Also, I woke up this morning with a sense of foreboding in regards to your sister, Ms. Bina, and Yona."

"Yona? Is something going on with Yona?" Jessah asked in concern.

"Not to worry, child," Miss Haddie reassured her. "I am already planning to visit Bina this evening and she will inform me as to what is going on. I too woke up with that same sense, but I know there is plenty of time for us to address this situation, whatever it is."

"Oh good. I feel much better about that. I don't want anything to happen to either Ms. Bina or Yona," Jessah answered. Turning once again towards Oren, Miss Haddie let him know that they could discuss this further after she spoke with her sister.

"Good! Well, now that I have eaten, I think I might rest up a little more before I get sent out again on my next assignment." With that, Oren stood up and headed back out the door to the guest home where he now resided.

Miss Haddie stood and encouraged Jessah to assist her in cleaning up a little, even as her heart silently cried out to Elemet for the wisdom they all needed in assisting their friends.

Chapter Twenty-Four

HURDLES AND COMPLICATIONS

As Shoshanna woke up that morning, her first thought was recalling the comment Galen had made to her prior to their entry through the fiery curtain. He called her "the bravest woman he had ever met." That certainly encouraged her, but what really got her thinking was his expressed desire to get to know her a little bit better once they arrived at the Eagles' Nest.

That idea was definitely intriguing, but without knowing what the Eagles' Nest was like, it would be hard to imagine developing a deeper friendship with Galen. She wanted time to explore their new residence and get to know the people who obviously already lived there. Staying focused on one man might be a little challenging, but after getting settled there, she felt that there might be a possibility of a more intense relationship. She would have to see what happens.

The idea of having a say in whom she might consider for marriage was a very new concept to her and there was no way she was going to rush into that without examining all her options. Who knows, there might be some young man there at the Eagles' Nest that might capture her attention even more than Galen. Only time would tell.

After concluding her own personal counseling session, she decided it was time to get up. Though still a little early, she was anxious to take a better look around with the morning sunlight illuminating their surroundings.

Pulling back the flap of her tent, Shoshanna poked her head out confirming that she was indeed the first one awake. As she crawled out, she noticed the fire had grown cold and needed to be stoked so they could enjoy a hot cup of tea along with their breakfast. Looking around, she found some small branches suitable for kindling and gathered them up.

As she walked around scanning the ground for more wood, she suddenly heard a rustling in the branches above her and looked up. Her eyes grew large as she saw a number of huge golden eagles assembled in the branches above and sitting on the precipices surrounding the entrance to the canyon before them.

Startled, she screamed and dropped the kindling. By the time she reached the tents, all three of the young men were up and staring wide-eyed at the massive birds with their sharp talons and meat-tearing beaks gazing down upon them.

Instinctively, Shoshanna ran over towards Galen, grabbing his arm for protection. No one said anything for a time as the observant eagles and worried travelers carefully studied each other.

"I wonder if we are breakfast," Roany whispered to his companions.

"Well, if they think they are going to start ripping on me, I can promise you, it won't be without a fight!" Uri said as he pushed up his sleeves in preparation for a battle. Waving his arms around, he tried his best to scare the massive birds off. "Get out of here! Go home! We are not your breakfast!"

Though a few of the birds flapped their wings briefly, none of them left their perches but continued watching the travelers with undeterred focus.

While Uri tried his best to scare the birds off, Galen noticed something different about these birds of prey. As he listened, he thought he heard a deep guttural sound, barely noticeable, as if they were communicating with each other.

"Do you hear that?" he asked the others. "It sounds like chatter coming from the birds, though I can't really decipher it. I really think they might be speaking to each other." Shoshanna released Galen's arm and took one step closer to the surrounding eagles, focusing in on their intense eyes. As she stared, she recognized a slight glow around their bodies, a light she had grown quite familiar with.

"Maybe they are friends, and not predators at all," she proposed. "Remember Jessah's story about flying on the back of that golden eagle? What if these eagles are the same type as that eagle?"

"Is there more than one friendly eagle on Kumani?" Roany wondered out loud.

"They obviously have not yet swooped down on us. That is good." Galen said while carefully studying the congregated birds. "Let's see what they do when we start packing up. Maybe they will just get bored and move on."

Cautiously, the group gathered up their supplies, tents, and blankets as the watchful eyes of the eagles remained focused on them. None of the travelers felt much like eating breakfast while the potentially hungry birds stared them down. Their stomachs were already in knots, so Galen just offered each of his companions a cold biscuit for them to munch on. Before them laid the steep canyon with very little room for a quick retreat if that was needed. Once everything was ready, the group moved ahead in single file warily entering the canyon.

They hoped once they started moving, the eagles would lose interest and fly to investigate other things. Unfortunately, they did not scatter, but rather followed the group's progression flying from precipice to precipice directly overhead.

"It's like they are guarding this place," Shoshanna whispered to the others.

"I think you're right, Shoshanna," Galen replied. "I wish I could understand what they are saying to each other. It might make me feel a little better."

"Or, it might make you feel a whole lot worse! They're not taking their eyes off us," Uri said, "that is for sure."

"Rather than focusing on the eagles, why don't we just focus on where we are going," Galen suggested. "We've learned so much about not allowing fear or worry to dominate our thoughts. I say, just ignore them. We will be fine."

Taking a deep breath, each of them made every effort to disregard their presence so they could focus on what was before them. Once Shoshanna released her nervousness about the eagles, she noticed beautiful veins of gold running through the stones lining the steep canyon they were walking through. Running her hands along the cold boulders, each time her hand passed over one of the streaks, she felt a charge of energy surge through her body.

"Have any of you noticed the gold veins embedded into the canyon walls?" she asked. The other three, taking a moment to also examine the stones around them, ran their hands over the glistening gold veins they had not previously noticed.

"Do you feel that surge when you touch the gold?" she inquired.

"Yes!" Roany admitted. "What is that?"

"I'm not sure," Galen confessed. "I've never felt that before."

"Maybe it has something to do with being stuck in this narrow canyon," Shoshanna suggested. "I wonder if Elemet wants us to take notice of the beauty he has created even in hard places?"

"That gold is beautiful," Uri commented. "If only we had the time to dig it out! I could sure use that extra charge along the way."

"I'm not sure if we are supposed to carry that gold with us physically to get that charge we are feeling," Galen suggested. "I think this gold is here for anyone passing through this gorge just to encourage them."

"That makes sense," Shoshanna agreed. "If other people came through here like us after the long journey through the smoking mountains, they would certainly appreciate the encouragement as well. It's amazing how Elemet prepared all these things for us!"

Meanwhile, as the others were busy talking, Uri was working hard to chip off a little of the gold so he could keep it with him at all times. Try as he might, nothing could be broken off, so he soon gave up on his efforts. It was obviously not meant to be.

After the recharge of encouragement, the friends were finally ready to continue down through the gorge to whatever lay before them. The fear and nervousness had completely lifted to the point to where they were finally ready to nibble on their biscuits while continuing their trek.

Much more aware of their surroundings, they noticed and admired the other colorful stones imbedded in the walls as they walked by. The walk actually became more fun as they called out the varying colors and textures for the others to take notice of and enjoy.

As Shoshanna took her eyes off the trail briefly to look at other variations of stones, she neglected to notice a medium-sized stone lying in the path directly in front of her. She gave a cry out in pain as her ankle twisted causing her to fall to the ground. Within seconds, the three young men were at her side attempting to help.

"Are you all right?" Galen asked.

"I think so," she replied. "Maybe I just need a moment to catch my breath before I try getting up."

"This would be a good time for a lunch break, especially since we really didn't stop for breakfast," Galen suggested. Uri and Roany quickly responded by gathering up all the knapsacks and producing whatever food remained for everyone to eat while Galen remained at Shoshanna's side.

"May I look at your ankle, please?" Galen asked. Agreeing to his request, Shoshanna pulled up her skirt just enough so Galen could pull off her shoe. Once the shoe was removed, he could easily see the ankle was red and already beginning to swell.

"Hmm. Does it hurt if I press on it?" Shoshanna gave a short cry when Galen applied some pressure. "Ok. That is not good. I'm pretty sure your ankle is sprained. We may need to wrap it up before continuing on, and you will definitely need help. We don't know how much further we need to go through this gorge, so we will need to take it pretty slow."

"Well, if one of you is feeling some heat in your hands just like I experienced when Uri nearly fell, maybe I can be healed like he was. Anyone?" she asked. All three young men stopped what they were doing to see if any of their hands were glowing red indicating something uncommon was about to happen.

Nothing.

As there seemed to be little any of them could do for her swollen ankle, Galen tore off the edge from Shoshanna's underskirt and wrapped it as best he could. Once she was comfortable, the four sat on nearby boulders to eat and consider what they needed to do next.

Chapter Twenty-Five

WHAT TO DO?

With their meal complete, Galen helped Shoshanna up to see if she could put any weight on her ankle. She could not. As it was obvious she was going to need assistance for the rest of their journey, the men figured out a system where two of them at a time would walk alongside her allowing her to place her arms around their necks as she hopped along.

The men would switch off every so often so that one of them could rest. However, Shoshanna soon learned that hopping on one leg was exhausting, even with the assistance of her friends, so she only managed to go a short distance before she needed to rest.

After watching Galen and Roany struggle to assist Shoshanna only a short distance, Uri had enough. Once they stopped to allow Shoshanna to rest, Uri stepped in. With his large arms and Shoshanna's more petite size, Uri had no problem sweeping her up into his arms and carrying her as they passed through the canyon.

As they walked, Shoshanna felt a little bad at becoming such a burden to her friends, especially Uri.

"I hope I'm not too heavy for you to carry," she said, a little embarrassed at the turn of events.

"You don't have to worry about that," he assured her with a smile. "I was made strong for a reason. Besides, your hands brought healing to me a while back, so now my hands can carry you. It's only fair."

Shoshanna smiled back at her friend. Yes, she had indeed been blessed with the perfect friends to bring her along on this difficult journey. Glancing over at Galen and Roany, now forced to carry two knapsacks each, she was impressed with all their willingness to take on extra burdens just to help a friend in need. They were all amazing, she decided.

Fortunately, the trail they were following had grown wider allowing them to walk next to each other with much more ease, so they were all able to talk and visit with each other as they walked.

Roany, who determined it was time to reminisce, posed a question for each of them to answer.

"In looking back over this entire journey we have been on, which portion did you find the most difficult?" Galen was the first to respond.

"Oh, that is easy! It was when I found myself surrounded by wolves near the apple tree. I thought for sure it was over for me!"

"And it would have been if it hadn't been for Chen showing up when he did, right?" Shoshanna added.

"Right!" Galen agreed. "I learned a big lesson about giving over to fear and worry at that time. And speaking of fear, have you noticed the eagles are not following us anymore?" At the mention of the eagles, everyone looked up confirming that the great birds were certainly gone.

"Once we got distracted with all the colorful stones, we completely forgot about them!" Roany laughed. "They must have gotten bored when we weren't giving them any more attention. Ok, Uri. Your turn. What was your most difficult challenge?"

"For sure, it was when I allowed hunger to make unwise decisions for me. I can't believe I decided to climb down that rocky hillside just to get a few apples. Dumb and painful for sure!"

"Yeah, that was pretty rough until Shoshanna's hands healed you," Roany agreed.

"Actually, it was not my hands that healed him," Shoshanna corrected him. "It was Elemet's gift that healed him."

"Very true!" Roany responded.

"And how about you?" Galen asked. "What was your most challenging time?"

"Oh, without question, it was when my head felt like it was going to explode that one time early in the journey. Do you remember?" Roany asked.

"Of course I remember!" Galen replied. "I had you surrender to Elemet so you could be under his protection and be able to resist all those terrible thoughts. That was pretty intense, I have to admit."

"Now Shoshanna, it's your turn," Roany stated. "What was the most challenging part of this journey so far? Let me guess! When you sprained your ankle!"

Smiling at Roany, she responded. "Actually, though that was quite painful, probably the hardest part of this whole journey was having to leave my father just as that mob was coming to arrest us. Though Chen assured me he was taken care of, I still wonder at times what happened with him?"

As they were walking considering all the challenges they had already been through, they suddenly realized that a fifth person had joined them on their trek. Chen was walking in their midst. Once they noticed him, they wanted to stop, but Chen encouraged them to keep walking as he spoke.

"My friends, I am so proud of how you have grown while overcoming all these challenges. Though the walk has been long and tiring at times, many sweet things have been deposited in each of you throughout this journey and have helped prepare you for this new season that is before you."

"First, just because you asked, Shoshanna, I will be happy to tell you what has become of Oren, your father. As you escaped, your father escaped as well by passing through the thorny hedge created to protect you all. He found his way to Miss Haddie's home and has since become a powerful advocate for Elemet and the way of the eagle. As his cabin was burned down by the enforcers, he now resides in a guest house on Miss Haddie's homestead when he is not out in the woods delivering messages and helping others. He is known as "the Woodsman" among those he serves." Shoshanna was amazed and taken by surprise at the changes in her father.

Next, Chen addressed Galen. "Galen, I know you have had concerns for your parents from time to time, but let me assure you, they are very happy and are doing well in their new position."

"New position?" Galen was clearly puzzled.

"Yes, thanks to Oren, they were warned about the spy planted as a friend and helper to them. Once they realized that they were to be used as 'bait' to assist in recapturing you, they decided to leave and destroy their own home so it would not draw you into a trap. As they left, I met with them. They are now happily protected living on their new homestead which can be used to assist others on their way to the Eagle's Nest."

"Really?" Galen asked. "They know both you and Elemet now?"

"They do!" Then Chen turned his attention to Roany. Chen could see Roany's feelings of guilt overcome him as he thought about the mother he left behind. She had caused much loss and turmoil in the lives of his friends.

"Roany, I have wonderful news for you. Though your mother was an enemy to the way of the eagle at one time, she has made an amazing turnaround. I met with her and we discussed her ways and her life. Being stricken with blindness for a time did help, I must admit. However, once she surrendered, Oren was able to forgive her and then use his gift to release Tanzi from her blindness. Now she sits awaiting further instructions for her next assignment."

"My mother was blind?" Roany asked.

"Yes, but now she can really see!" Chen responded.

"And my father was involved with that as well?" Shoshanna inquired.

"He most certainly was!" Chen replied. "You see, not only have all of you changed, but the ones you left behind have changed as well because you trusted me to take care of them."

Uri had grown quite silent as the others rejoiced in the good news of their families, but Chen had not forgotten him.

"Uri, I know you have spent much of your time growing up feeling quite alone in life, but I want to assure you that once you move into the Eagles' Nest, all that will change. You will discover a new family that loves and embraces you like never before. In fact, I think you have already met a few of them!" Uri looked around at his new friends. Yes, he had to admit, he really did have the beginning of a beautiful new family!

Suddenly, the path came to a dead end with no exit in sight. Sheer stone walls surrounded them on three sides. Chen, without commenting on their sudden halt, simply instructed Uri to put Shoshanna down allowing her to stand up. At first, he objected stating that her ankle could not handle the weight, but Chen just nodded at him with a smile.

As Uri assisted Shoshanna in standing up, she discovered that her ankle no longer hurt and she was able to walk freely as if she had never twisted her ankle at all! While they were all rejoicing, they noticed that Chen was no longer in their midst. After looking around, Galen came to the conclusion that somehow they must be at the end of their journey.

"Let's begin examining the walls around us," he encouraged them. "There must be a hidden door somewhere. I'm sure Chen would not leave us here without a way to enter in."

As they studied every crack they could see, Shoshanna suddenly felt a wisp of fresh air from a portion of the rock she had her hand on. Calling the others over, they all joined her in feeling the stones all around it. Suddenly, when Shoshanna gave the stone a slight push, it moved.

"I think we may have arrived," she announced as the stone slowly moved. The great stone door opened up before Shoshanna revealing a whole new life and experience for each of them. The beauty and splendor of the Eagle's Nest took their breath away as they stepped into the beginnings of their new destinies as residents and warriors of freedom.

OTHER BOOKS BY MARY TRASK

 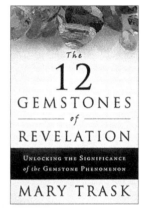

www.heartreflectionsministries.com

mary@heartreflectionsministries.com

CPSIA information can be obtained
at www.ICGtesting.com
Printed in the USA
FSHW011330140519
58129FS

9 781545 663691